Mercury Blobs

All over the place in the space of a mind

Sylvia Petter

First published in Australia
by
RAGING AARDVARK PUBLISHING
http://ragingaardvark.com

ISBN: 0-9871383-7-5
ISBN-13: 978-0-9871383-7-8

Cover Images: © Sharon Ratheiser
Cover Design by Sessha Batto

Raging Aardvark Publishing.
Brisbane, Australia
Established 2012

What they said about The Past Present:

"..a good mix of thought-provoking work, leavened by the occasional humorous piece. All in all, this is a very strong first collection."

–Zoe King, Editor, Buzzwords Magazine, UK.

What they said about Back Burning, Best Fiction Award at IP Australia, 2007:

"Sylvia Petter is a cartographer of dislocated lives. With compassionate precision, she charts the detours, the disruptive incursions of passion, loneliness and loss, the ever-shifting conceptions of home and of the self. Her characters are always on the move through complicated terrain, and the journey is richly rewarding for the reader."

–Janette Turner Hospital, prizewinning author of the short story collection, *Forecast: Turbulence*

What they said about Mercury Blobs:

"The brilliant stories in Sylvia Petter's *Mercury Blobs* are sometimes very funny and sometimes very moving, and often they are both at once, which is one of the best tests of a truly serious writer. Moreover, she is a master of the very short fictional forms that have become a crucial expressive medium of the 21st-century sensibility. This is a splendid collection from a gifted writer

–Robert Olen Butler, author of the Pulitzer Prize-winning *A Good Scent from a Strange Mountain*.

ACKNOWLEDGEMENTS

"Widow's Peak" was first published in both the print and online versions of *Southern Ocean Review* (New Zealand, 1997) and was subsequently included in the Duckworth (UK) anthology, *Valentine's Day—women against men: Stories of Revenge*, ed. Alice Thomas Ellis, in the 2000 and 2001 editions. Twenty very short pieces were written for the *Your Messages Project* conducted online in November 2007 by Sarah Salway and Lynne Rees; "Chicle Alert" appeared in the *Your Messages* anthology (Bluechrome, UK, 2008). "Baku" appeared in the September 2012 issue of *World Literature Today* and "Anna's Flags" appeared in *Bridges: A Global Anthology of Short Stories*, ed. Maurice A. Lee (Tenemos Publishing, North Little Rock, 2012). Variations of "Uncle Henri" have appeared in Flash Flood and *Twisted Tales* (Raging Aardvark, Australia, 2012/2013). Variations of other stories have appeared in R*eading for Real* (Canada), *FreeXpression* and *Unsweetened* (Australia), *Beginnings* (USA) and *Offshoots* and *Ex Tempore* (Switzerland), in various charity anthologies, and at *Ether Books*.

I should like to thank *Outsapop* for inspiring "Trashion Passion", and our daughter, Maarit, for inspiring "The Memory Box". I should also like to thank Sharon Ratheiser who provided the artwork for *The Past Present, Back Burning* and now *Mercury Blobs*.

I am grateful to Nik Perring for his editorial advice, and to Sessha Batto for the book cover design.

To Günter,

for letting me raid his dreams and for never complaining about all the mercury blobs.

CONTENTS

FIRST LOVE

He donned a brown pair of trousers, a white shirt and a green woollen jacket. He glanced in the large gold-sculpted mirror and pulled the brim of his felt hat deep into his face. He left through a back door and slipped out into the streets of Vienna.

He walked through back alleys and for the first time in his life he felt free. Down by the market there was a baker. Through the window he saw her. She was the one. Had to be. He entered and asked for some bread. She pushed a large brown loaf towards him, but averted her eyes. He offered a note. She had no change.

"What's all this?" said her father.

"It's an advance," he said and then added: "For all the loaves I'm still going to buy."

She smiled. Warm rouge crept over her cheeks. Her eyes were bright as she nodded a "Thank you". Her father said nothing.

Her flushed smile stayed with him and kept his heart light as he sat on the bench outside the bakery. He waited and watched. Then she came out. He walked with her through the back streets. The next day they walked by the banks of the Danube. The one after, he kissed her.

State business took him to Budapest, but his heart stayed in Vienna. When he came back after a month, he found the bakery boarded up. The whole family's gone, they told him. Where to, they didn't know, they said. But he noticed how they averted their eyes. How they would not linger. He felt so alone.

He found her dead in the hospice. He sat by her bed, held her white hand and sobbed. The nun shook her head and looked away. It wasn't Mayerling. That was yet to come.

WIDOW'S PEAK

Jean-Pierre tipped my head back in the basin and started the warm water running. "I'm sorry to hear about your husband," he said.

I didn't answer.

"So sudden," he added. "Was it his heart?"

"Yes," I said quietly as he rubbed a cool thick liquid over my hair.

"You don't have to talk about it," he said. "How about a midnight blue tint to cover the odd grey, add a little glamour?"

"For a widow? That wouldn't be right."

"You have to look after yourself. Life goes on," Jean-Pierre said and massaged my head.

Yes, it does, Jean-Pierre. If only you knew. Yes, it was his heart that killed him. He shouldn't have split it in two. A heart attack. He'd always had a weak heart. I think it was because I thought he was simulating. I wasn't of course, so I had to attack and I killed him in bed.

I didn't kill them all in bed, of course. Then, not being married, it wouldn't have been right. Anyway, I was far too young the first time.

I was ten and Wayne Smuthers eleven. It was just when school was about to break up and he'd asked me to go down the bush.

"What for?" I said.

"Show you the gorge.'""

"I've been there," I said.

"Not the place I know. Scaredy cat!"

"I am not!"

"Come on then."

The bush was thick there and huge rocks littered the creek, as if they'd been thrown down by some angry god who'd lost at a game of jacks. They'd made crevices I'd slip into and sometimes I'd worry I'd get stuck and die a slow starving death. Higher up there were caves, but I was never allowed to climb up to them.

"You going to one of the caves?"

Wayne didn't answer and just held out his hand. No boy had ever held out his hand to me before, well not when he didn't have to, so I took it.

"I'm game," I said and felt a funny shivery feeling.

No one saw us go down the back of the school and then across to where the blue gums start getting thick. They look like tall skinny soldiers and you can hear birds and lizards scuttling, but you hardly see any. When we got to the gorge, Wayne let go of my hand. "It's up there," he said, pointing past the last boulder to a high rock platform in the rock face.

"We'll never make it," I said.

"Yes, we will. Follow me."

Wayne easily slipped through the crevice in the rock face, but I had to hold my breath so I wouldn't get stuck. There were some footholds, but they didn't look natural.

"You make those?" I asked.

"Took ages," he said proudly. He was halfway up the rock face on the inside of the crevice. "Come on. You can't fall. Just lean on the rock as you go up."

I was puffing by the time I hoisted myself on to the ledge in front of the cave. "So?"

"In the cave," he said.

"I don't want to. Looks creepy."

"Scaredy cat," he said again and went in. So I followed.

An earthy smell of yeast came from the dark cave. "Lets go home," I said.

"Not yet," he said and put his arm out barring my way at the entrance. "Bet you've never been kissed."

I wasn't going to let on. "I have so!" I said.

5

"Bet you don't even know how," he said.

I wanted to run, but that funny feeling kept coming back. "I do so."

"So prove it," he said and flattened me against the wall. And then his wet mouth clamped on mine like he was almost swallowing me.

"Get out!" I yelled and pushed back as hard as I could, but he just squashed me against the rock. "I'm going to show you. No one else will," he said as he pinned back my arms.

I put my head up and tried to move my mouth away from his. "What do you mean?"

"You're just a fat goggle-eyed catfish. It's your last chance," he said, grinning.

The evening sky was bleeding red through the treetops as I shoved him back. I couldn't believe my own strength and he tumbled to the edge of the ledge and rolled off. I was still shaking as I spat out the mouldy taste of him and wiped my glasses on my skirt. He'd just disappeared. Flown away. Gone. And then I heard him screaming.

"I'm stuck. Help! Get me out!"

I crawled to the edge. Wayne was pinned down in the crevice and blood was all over his face and arms. I squinted at him. He looked like a snow gum with his white arms and legs and the sticky red glistening on him like resin. He looked almost beautiful. Just seeing him like that made me feel so calm, happy even. I scrambled down the crevice wall and when I was just out of touching distance I saw there was no way I could get him out.

"Get help!" he whimpered. "Please."

By the time the search party found him three days later he was dead. When I heard all the grownups clucking about how Wayne could never keep out of the gorge, I just remember thinking he'd lost his bet. It was all his own fault, wasn't it?

"Not too hot?" Jean-Pierre asked as he rinsed the shampoo.

I gave a slight shake of my head. "Some nourishment," he said as he spread a cool liquid over my scalp. "I'll leave it five minutes."

My puppy fat melted, I started wearing contact lenses and learnt how to kiss. But it never seemed what my girlfriends made it out to be.

At least not until I met Enzo.

Enzo was the purser on a cruise ship up North and one of his jobs was to organise show time. He'd get all the girls up on deck and make us practise the Can-Can. After practice, he'd take me for a drink in the bar and then back to his cabin. He showed me how to kiss all right and lots of other things, but I always held back. He said he loved me, so I thought he could wait. But I didn't know he'd said the same thing to all the girls on that ten-day cruise.

I remember the day we had the show almost pat and he decided we had to finish the finale with a Catherine wheel. All the other girls managed it first go, but I was scared I'd go over the edge and I balked every time.

"Your rhythm's all wrong," Enzo said. "Haven't you got any soul, any passion?" And he pushed me aside and said to one of the girls, a tall leggy brunette who'd always been giving him the hairy eyeball: "You show her!"

The brunette sprang a perfect wheel. "Now you do it," he said to me.

"I can't," I said. Tears welled in my eyes and I thought my contacts would fall out. So I went over to lean on the railing.

"Watch me, then," he said to my back.

I turned around. He seemed to pull himself in like elastic, then almost bouncing off one foot he careered straight at me. I gripped the railing and, just as he was in flight, even lifting his hands from the deck floor, I felt the railing loosen behind me and I pulled myself to one side.

Enzo went over the edge. He'd done exactly what I'd been scared of doing and landed in the ocean. They tried to save him, but it was a long way down and as he was going head over heels, he must have split his skull on the hull, and then there was the propeller… A bloody mess. I was shattered of course, but he had come on strong, and he'd betrayed and humiliated me.

After that, all the screws on the boat were checked so that no more could become loose—not even through twiddling.

Jean-Pierre rinsed my head with cool water.

"The tint has to take, just relax," he said as the smell of the colour piqued my nostrils.

I was about to give up on men when I met number three.

He was a nice enough chap, but he had that spiel with all his problems. Of course, he was married, but I only found that out later. So to show him how broad-minded I was, I cooked him a meal - filet mignon with mushroom sauce.

It's really so hard to tell "death cap" mushrooms from the real thing. It was when I saw all the attention his widow got, why, she was coddled and feted, and then her life started, that I decided to find a husband all my own. Stability, that's what I wanted. And marriage did confer a certain respectability.

"Just a few minutes more," Jean-Pierre said as I started to fidget in my chair.

But number four still wasn't Mr Right. He was single all right, but just as I had at last reached full flame he suddenly cooled off.

Unrequited love and a woman's scorn can be such a deadly mixture. As we'd been close I, of course, knew all about his allergy. But was it my fault that I'd forgotten to take the bowl of beer from under the balcony table? Was it my fault that the wasps got angry when he kicked the bowl over? Was it my fault that I couldn't find his injection pack of antidotes soon enough after they'd attacked him?

Jean-Pierre rinsed my head quickly and then covered it in a soft fluffy towel. "Move over in front of the mirror while I put in the rollers," he said.

I watched him intently as he worked, parting and twirling my long jet hair until my head was covered in a crown of glistening black coils. "The infra-red dryer for a few more minutes and then you'll see the new you," he said and smiled at my face in the mirror.

I blew him a kiss and settled back.

Number five was the one. He wined me and dined me and we soon tied the knot. He was very gentle and calm and disliked too much effort, pleading his heart. Nobody's perfect, I thought and so far he'd come closest to my idea of what was right. Why, he loved seeing me trip round the house with my duster, flicking the russet feathers over each fragile figurine. I had to admit as the years came and went that I enjoyed married life.

I can't recall when I first got suspicious. It must have been when he kept talking about his heart, but the medical exams all seemed very normal, normal for him and the state he'd been used to. But one day, it was at the end of February, the florist's bill arrived. The flowers for Valentine's had been delightful, but two bunches? That's when I started snooping around. The two-timing bastard! My husband, a bigamist. No wonder his heart had always been weak.

Jean-Pierre rolled away the dryer and began unravelling my hair from the foam rubber coils. I loved the way he brushed it out and, he was right, it shone and glimmered in the spotlights.

When I decided to kill my husband, I saw it as a charitable gesture. Two for the price of one, with the twist that I'd be helping a sister. And the word "widow" has such a respectable ring to it. But I had to be careful; the last thing I wanted in my nice tidy house was a mess. Of course, it needed a lot of preparation, let's call it a foreplay of sorts at which I had become expert. The diagnosis was heart attack from overexertion. His widow, the other one, came to the funeral and while she paid her condolences, which I had to return, I'm sure I caught a slight nod of approval.

"The style is just wonderful. Out of this world!" I said.

"You really should get out more," Jean-Pierre said. "Do you know how to dance?"

I nodded, admiring how he'd pulled back my hair, how it looked like black silk falling softly to my shoulders, framing my face in a perfect heart shape.

"There's a night club at the Holiday Inn. Lonely men go there to talk and whirl ladies round the floor," he said, spraying Gossamer in the air just above my head. "Younger ones, too," he added with a wink.

I stood and twirled in front of the mirror. Then I kissed Jean-Pierre on the cheek and gave him a generous tip. I knew he was right, there was so much to live for.

And besides, I'd never married a hairdresser.

CHUBBY GOES TO YALE

Chubby didn't want to go to Yale. In fact, he didn't want to go to any university, even though his parents had been putting money aside against tertiary dreams as long as he could remember. Chubby wanted to get a job, get money, and he wanted it now.

"You'll get a better job if you study. Education is the key, Chubby," his mother said.

"You're so fifties, Mom. And quit calling me Chubby."

"But you are, dear."

He heard those words every time he jumped on the scales and craned over his belly to see his weight. Right. He would quit eating. He would go on a hunger strike until they gave in and then they'd have to call him something else. Chubb sounded cool. When he was Chubb he'd go and look for a job.

"I'm going to become a locksmith," he said when he was 20 pounds lighter.

"Chu-ubb!"

"It's good money, and I can moonlight."

"That's against the law."

"Gotta catch me first, Mom. Nobody'll see me in the dark."

"What are we going to do about him?" his mother said to his father.

"Let him fall on his face. There's no money in making keys. They're a dime a dozen at the hardware store. He'll come round."

Chubb got a job at the hardware store. Nights he'd go out with his tools and pick locks. He'd never steal anything, but his boss marvelled at the run on padlocks. Everyone in town wanted one. He gave Chubb a raise, and in a few weeks another. Soon Chubb was rolling in it.

One day Chubb came home and said: "I've quit."

"Why?" said his mother.

"I'm going to Yale. Gonna get myself an MBA."

His father laughed. "Told you he'd come round."

"How about a triple hamburger, Mom?"

THE BURKA

She was swathed in black. All I could see were her eyes. She asked if she could have my used tea bag. I nodded and gestured that she might sit down. She said she could wait. Asked, could she wait? I nodded again and sipped my tea.

We were alone in the old cafe. Alone except for the elderly waiter who now approached us. Just water, she said. Plain.

Plain she was not. At least not those eyes.

Why do you want my tea bag? I asked.

I´m an artist, she said. I recycle.

I had a vision of a woman in a burka on a bike, swinging old teabags.

Performance?

She laughed.

The waiter placed a tumbler of water before her on the small round table separating us. She took hold of the glass and lifted her veil. She drank and placed the glass, one-third empty, or two-thirds full, back on the table.

I dry them and create collages with the tea and the scraps of bag. I even use the staples and the string.

It wasn´t my opinion of art.

My works are beautiful. And they sell, she said.

I´d like to see.

But can you? Her eyes were laughing.

I lifted the teabag from my cup. Laid it on the side of the saucer.

Squeeze it, she said.

With the back of my spoon I squeezed as much liquid as I could from the teabag and placed the spoon back on the saucer. There was a slight tinkle before it became still. I slipped my hand under the table and gripped my knee.

With two fingers she took the teabag by the string and held it to her nose. Darjeeling, she said, and pulled my paper napkin to her side of the table and placed the teabag onto it.

I shrugged. Tea was tea.

Oh, no. There are all different sorts, she said. Generic is an illusion.

But you.

Me?

I mean, all in black.

You mean, my burka?

Yes. I had been avoiding any mention of the black garment. I was open-minded. I had nothing against burkas. If that was the way these women wanted to dress. It did draw attention to their eyes. She did have lovely eyes. In a way, it was a change from the exposed breasts and tight pants, short skirts, and teetering heels that had become daily fare on my way to the office at the Ministry. I didn´t agree with the ban in the works. No burkas in public. Funny, that. Their men welcomed no burkas at home, I imagined. They wanted to see their luxurious hair, their bodies, their smiles. I would have liked to have seen her smile.

You mean my burka? She repeated.

Yes, I said.

Does it excite you? Make you wonder?

No. Yes.

Do you think that all women who cover themselves are the same?

I hesitated. They all did look the same. All that black. Just the eyes. But her eyes, they were lovely. They glistened and there was something provocative, teasing, in their look.

Do you?

I cleared my throat. With a fingernail she was dislodging the tea from one end of the bag.

I imagine.

What do you imagine?

I shifted in my seat. I imagine that you have long luxurious hair.

Is that all?

Yes. Of course.

Why?

Because. I cleared my throat again. I read somewhere that your hair is sacred. In your world, I mean.

Suddenly she looked around. The cafe was still empty. The waiter was nowhere to be seen. She quickly pushed back the black material from her head and slipped open her veil.

Nefertiti!

Cancer, she said. But I´m on the mend. Then she readjusted her burka and veil.

My heart was thumping so loudly, I was sure she could hear.

Your face is flushed, she said. Your heart must be pounding.

I thought. I imagined. I mean. I´ve never actually spoken to ...

A woman like me?

Yes.

Would you like another cup of tea?

I breathed steadily. Will you join me?

I do need the teabags, she said. Her eyes were laughing again. Perhaps mint, this time? For the contrast?

The contrast? I'd had about enough contrast for one day. I looked into her eyes and then nodded weakly. I motioned the waiter to bring two mint teas.

My name is Hawwa, she said. It is like your Eve.

I started to laugh and then stopped.

What is so funny?

Nothing, I said as the scent of mint wafted to our table.

We squeezed our teabags and I passed mine, now steadily, towards her saucer and gently laid it down.

My name is Adam. Generic is an illusion, I thought.

It really is, she said.

I stared at her.

I see you can see now, she said. Then she slipped a business card from the folds in her burka and pushed it across the table to me. My exhibition will be next month. This is the gallery. I would love to see you there.

I would love to see you, I thought as I took the card and put it in my wallet.

There'll be refreshments, she said. The only teabags will be in my art.

Then she placed a small metal box on the table and slipped the three teabags inside it, nodded at me, rose and left.

I watched her black silhouette leave the cafe, watched her disappear. Then I brought my cup of mint tea close to my nose and breathed in deeply.

BLACK COFFEE

She was sure she had seen him somewhere before. Her stare caught his eye and she quickly focused on her tea cup.

He was making straight for her table. "May I sit here?" he asked.

"Yes," she answered and continued to sip her tea. Her hand brushed an invisible strand of blonde hair from across her forehead.

It was half past eight in the evening and the small Geneva cafe was crowded as always on a Thursday night. Courses had just finished and some overtime workers had come for a warming drink before taking the bus home. She was one of the latter. There were only a few free seats left. One of them was at her table for two.

He smiled, took off his dark green raincoat and sat down. He turned his head as he arranged the coat neatly over the back of the chair and she could see that his dark curly hair just scraped the nape of his neck. He was not what one would call good-looking in the film star way but he had something that inspired confidence, an aura of charm. She could imagine him stretched out in an old-fashioned armchair in front of a burning hearth, a mug of tea in his hand. Where was it? It can't have been too long ago. He seems so familiar.

At times she travelled for work, at others for pleasure. For months on end she wouldn't budge; then there would be weeks of a suitcase life. Recently she had spent four days in Rome at a meeting, two days in Paris on the way there and a long weekend in London just getting away from it all. 'Away from what?' she wondered.

"Are the buses running on time?" he asked in English.

She started. Oh, my *Herald Tribune*, she thought. That's why he's speaking English. The paper lay folded on the table next to her cup, but the distinctive logo was still visible.

"Yes," she replied. "Swiss timing; the clocks, you know."

He smiled again and looked around for the waitress.

Wherever it was, she felt she knew that smile so well. A forgotten lover? Impossible. A gaze across the shelves at Waterstone's in London? It can't have been Rome, nor Paris. I would have remembered an English-speaker there.

He ordered black coffee. The plumpish waitress with her little white apron placed the steaming cup before him on the table. He sighed, drinking in the aroma, then gently closed his hand around the cup as if to draw out its warmth. Although she preferred tea she thought there must be something to coffee for him to almost purr the way he did.

I feel I've known him for ages, but I haven't even met him yet. Or have I? she thought. She glanced at her watch; the silver second hand was gliding. I'll have to run, she thought. I'll miss the bus. She stood up and slipped on her black redingote.

She could feel his eyes on her as she buttoned it up.

"Don't I know you from somewhere?" she ventured, her thoughts racing as she heard the words. It sounded like a pass; the usual line, just round the other way. She had to know but she had to go. If she missed her bus she would have to wait another thirty minutes for the next one.

"It's quite possible," he nodded and smiled up at her.

"But you're not from here?"

"No, but I come often and I stay a while."

She knew there was more to it than that but felt no wiser. The bus was pulling around the corner. "I have to go, good-bye," she blurted.

The orange and white bus pulled in to the stop still half a block past the café. She tried to sprint in her tight grey skirt, her black high heels clicking almost tripping down the asphalt. Her hair was flying. She wished she had been in jeans rather than her smart office gear. She arrived panting at the stop to see the bus pull off. 'Blast! Swiss timing! Just when I need it least. Or?'

23

The beginning of a smile teased her lips as she turned on her heels and made her way back to the café, breathing deeply. She straightened her skirt that had twisted to one side and brushed her long hair back from her forehead with her hand. Another twenty minutes to find out. Not just the run had blushed her cheeks. She opened the café door and parted the heavy curtain that kept out the draught. The café was less crowded. She looked toward her table. The cups were still there. He was gone.

"Heavens, I forgot to pay for my tea!" She was sitting down at her chair when the waitress came to clear the table.

"I'm sorry, I forgot to pay."

"The *monsieur* has paid," said the waitress. "What will it be?"

"Oh, another tea, please. Do you know where he went?"

"*Non*, he just left the right change. I didn't see him leave," she said making off to get the order.

Slipping her coat from her shoulders she leaned back in resignation. The waitress brought her tea and she took a sip.

It tasted like hot brown water. I should have tried coffee, black coffee, she thought. How could I have forgotten him? That smile, that calm, that comfort

Like a detective she tried to reconstruct her long weekend in London. She had stayed a while at the passport control replying to all sorts of questions, so many for just a long weekend. Then there had been lunch with her friend Susan, trying to fit in two years of news over a one-hour pizza. Had he been at the next table? She wouldn't have noticed; she and Susan had been too engrossed in catching up with each other. I must find more time for my friends, my women friends, she thought. She groped through her mind for the slightest clue.

The brown water had cooled; she didn't want it. I might as well wait in the bus shelter, she thought. At least I won't risk missing the last bus. Mustn't forget to pay.

She left some coins on the table and pulled her coat up over her shoulders. At the café door she stopped and turned her head as if expecting to see him come out from behind the coat rack. She didn't have to run this time; she could walk to the bus shelter. Another five minutes, only five minutes to wait.

She felt as if she had just missed meeting an old friend she had wanted to see. She knew the feeling well, mostly when she had come back from a trip, regretting it had been too short. There never was enough time to spend with friends: something was always left unsaid, forgotten in the hurried gabble.

She sat down on the wooden bench in the shelter and let out a sigh. Stretching her shoulders to unload some invisible burden she leaned her head against the shelter wall, her eyes half closed. She could hear the bus pulling in to the stop. She opened her eyes.

From behind a cup of black steaming coffee, Colombia Brand, so knowing, so comforting, he smiled out at her from his armchair in the oversized advertisement on the side of the bus.

NAME OF THE ROSE

"What's in a name? That which we call a rose

By any other name would smell as sweet."

When Romeo tried to find out, she followed up with: "Wherefore art thou?"

The swain grumbled as he dusted himself off.

"Wherefore art thou, Romeo?" Juliet yelled.

"In the bloody rosebush."

"Huh?"

"The ladder fell down." And off he went to capitulate. "I'm a swain, see. Got work to do."

What's in a name, Bill pondered. Swain. Swan. Swoon. Who?

"Who is Sylvia, what is she?"

No swanning me, Sylvia thought. Here he goes getting me into trouble now. That's what you get when you stop a girl living in the woods. She can't see the trees for the roses. No one can spell that name, anyway. Slyvia. Salvia.

It's no fun getting called Saliva at school. Spit and dribble. Yuk. And then when you get older and apply for management jobs, they send you letters inviting you to an interview, expenses paid, but it's addressed to Silvio. Who? Yeah, so I wear tights and keep my hair long. They saw through it. "Sorry, we were expecting a man?" But they let me keep the change for the trip home. Home? Ah, back to the woods where the trees are covered with climbing roses. Substitute whatever you like for "rose", as long as it's fragrant. What's in a name? Try clothes.

Clothes make the man. What about women? Turn on the PC. Clothes make the person; any avatar on Second Life can tell you that. Have another go, Bill. They're working on making the roses smell. Scratch 'n' sniff. Don't need names. Just fly. Do. Be. Do-bee-do, as a mate of mine once said. Watch out for the sting, though, and the thorns that can scratch when you fall back into reality.

NECROPIX

"I need a control group," Annette said. She sat cross-legged on the floor, her elbows on her knees, her face propped in her hands.

"What's the subject?" I said, adoring her dilemma and her hair dipping to her shoulders, loving the way it almost hid one eye.

"Divorce rates."

"Done the rats already?"

"You're way behind, Wayne. We've got a new subject," she said and gave me a long look. "You're really not focussed, are you?"

I shrugged. "Maybe I'm focussed on things I like." I thought of the photos I'd shot of the rats. The best part was when they were trapped. When I was totally in control. "Anyway, I like the rats," I said.

"I know," she said and ruffled my hair. When she did that I wanted to spool hers through my fingers, but she always pulled back too soon.

I'd met my wife when we were both studying psychology. She was studying like it was an obsession. I was just dabbling, but the rats got me hooked. I was meant to be doing architecture, design and landscape gardening.

"So who do I get in my control group?" Annette said.

"On?"

"Marriage."

"Marriage?" I said. Marriage? I thought. I knew I'd get her one day.

"And divorce," she said.

I scratched my head. I don't remember the end of that conversation.

Annette must have finished her project. I hadn't noticed. I'd turned to landscaping.

We'd married straight after graduation. As time went by we felt things closing in on us. Little things. The pressures of finding the right niche. Maybe that was why we both went into the professions we have today. Maybe we thought that by attacking our fears up front, we could control them. Of course, we didn't know what we were doing back then.

My wife became a marriage counsellor. I'm what you could call a graveyard architect. I went from one architect's firm to another—urban planning, in a way. I moved ahead, going nowhere. And meanwhile Annette went back for her Ph.D. Once established, Annette would bring her work home. She'd go through some of the case studies with me. Ethics kept her from mentioning names.

"I'll have to suggest they split up," she said. "For their own good."

"Thought you were meant to keep them together," I said.

"Counsel is counsel." It was the last case she discussed with me.

We were sitting in our top-floor apartment one evening. I'd put my feet up on the Chesterfield. Annette was wearing her shocking pink power suit, her brand new heels still on her feet. She loved shoes. Started loving them when she went big time. When she put the plaque with "Dr Annette Parsons" on our letter box and front door. I turned on the CD player.

Cowboy Junkies. I listened to Annette with half an ear.

"When I think back to those control groups at uni."

"You mean the rats?" I said.

The Junkies sang the line about racing sunsets.

"Of course not!" she said. "What have they got to do with my work now?" She caressed the side of her shoe. Black kid.

"Rats and marriage counselling?" I said. "Yeah. You've got a point."

"Glad you can see it. The trouble I had getting my stats down back then ..."

I'd never noticed Annette ever having trouble with figures. She always managed to fit them the way she wanted. "Guess it's easier now. Isn't it? I mean those stats gave you a job. Didn't help me much though, did they?"

"I don't know. You were never serious about psychology. You just ..."

"Dabbled?"

"Yes. You dabbled," she said and stroked her tight skirt. "The way you still are."

"So that's what you think. After all this time. Well, if you're honest you know why I took Psych I."

"So why? Do tell." She fixed me with an innocent gaze.

"Come on, Annette." My eyes coasted over her trim silk shirt and the pattern of lace shining through. A pearl button had slipped from its hole just below her collarbone. "To be in your class."

Annette's fingers popped the pearl back in its buttonhole. Buttoned up. She seemed more and more so lately. That was the downside of racing after a career, I thought. She called it a vocation. Where had the time gone?

"So did the rats help?" she said and peaked an eyebrow sharply.

"They did in fact. I stuck with architecture, didn't I?"

"You call that architecture?"

"Doesn't always have to be buildings, does it?"

"But graves?" She drew her ankles together.

"I needed my niche, too," I said.

Annette pursed her lips.

I never brought my work home from the cemetery, which was natural. Talking about corpses and how to dispose of them isn't really something for a comfortable home life. But I had my problems, too. I had to find something new. A way out. Before my niche bogged me down. I'd had an idea.

"Not any old graves, Dr Parsons, I'll have you know." I'd call her Dr Parsons when she pissed me off. Knew she hated it, coming from me. "Vertical graves. Eternal canisters. Ecological. Space effective. Discreet."

"Discreet? With photos of the occupants on the top?"

"Names are there, too. Thought it was an innovative touch. And people like it," I said.

"Yes. I see how it could be successful. Just goes to show what things are coming to."

"What are things coming to? We both studied rats and we both got jobs out of it. If things hadn't gone that way ..." If things hadn't gone that way, where would we be now, I thought. Where are we now? "It wasn't so much about disposal per se, Dr Parsons. More about managing the cemetery grounds." I rose and went to the bar. "Whisky?" I said.

Annette shook her head.

I sat down again, empty handed. "I had to find room. Vertical graves. Tubes. With a portrait of the person on the top."

"That's sick," Annette said.

"They used to take photos of the open coffin in the old days. And it's good for Who's Who.'"

"Who IS who?" Annette said with a slight sneer in her voice.

"What do you mean?" I sipped my drink. "Names alone don't say anything. Photos help. Identifiers."

Annette raised both eyebrows. Said nothing.

"Christ, Annette! It's my work!"

"Yeah. But you don't have to apply it at home." Her gaze dropped onto the Nikon on the coffee table. I always had it at hand.

"You trying to tell me something?"

"Can't you see?"

"See what?"

Annette shrugged.

"Hey! Smile!" I grabbed the camera, focussed and shot.

Annette stuck out her tongue. "Wish you'd put that damn thing away. Gives me the creeps," she said.

"Very pretty," I said. "Portrait of Dr Annette Parsons, renowned marriage counsellor. Taken by her husband. Dr Parsons has the creeps."

"I'm not one of the candidates for your *Who's Who* collection," she said, got up and went to the kitchen.

I heard clinking.

"Want a drink?" she called.

"Yeah."

"What?" she said.

"Whatever you like."

"Tell me what?" Her voice climbed half an octave.

"Don't care," I said dully.

Annette came back with two glasses of white wine.

"I didn't want wine."

"Why didn't you say so?" she snapped.

I took the glass.

"Why don't you say what you want?" she said.

I shrugged. "You should know."

"How can I if you don't tell me." She pinned up a stray strand that had escaped from her chignon.

I shrugged again and sipped the wine. It was bitter. Sour. I swallowed. I watched her as she crossed her long legs. "New shoes again?" I said.

"What do you mean?"

"Tenth pair this quarter," I said running my eyes over the soft Italian leather.

"So? My money."

"Your fetish."

"Don't use that word lightly," she said. "You and your necropix, that's a fetish."

"That's my work. I save space with my tubular coffins planted upright. Why do you need new shoes every week? We'll soon have to move out. Or move to the cellar. You know what happened to Imelda M.?"

"Very funny!"

"Joke?" I raised my hands and turned my palms towards her. Annette's eyes fixed them, then rose to my face. Bullseye! I was unprepared for her next words.

"It's no good, Wayne," she said.

"What's no good?"

"Us," she said flatly.

"What do you mean?"

"It's not working."

"Then fix it. You're the expert." I swilled the wine in my glass.

"Wayne, it's over," Annette said. Then she stood up, placed her half-finished glass on the table and walked out.

I heard the door click shut. "I won't let you go!" I called, but she must have already been in the lift down. There was no way I'd let her go. That knot wouldn't cut in on us. We'd sworn to keep it away. Meet it head on. Work it all out. We knew what we were doing and Annette was the expert.

We'd joked about it before. At least I thought she'd been joking. I had been. I'd always thought it was easier that way. She'd said, "I want a divorce. You can't stop me." I'd said: "Yes, I can." What did she think she was doing now? Calling my bluff? I wasn't bluffing.

She'd be back. Like the other times. I'd tried to make it big time. She knew that. Her ethics would never allow her to leave me. We'd gone on too far together. Too long. I drained my glass. Anyway, she'd have to come back for her shoes. I'd be waiting.

Two weeks later when I came back from work I was tired as never before. It had been a hard day. Physically. Mentally. I had to unwind. I made myself a whisky on the rocks, the way I liked it. Then I stretched back and pulled out Annette's photo. She grimaced at me in black and white, her tongue sticking out.

My brain spun and then stopped cold. Yes. I really did kill her. It was amazingly easy. I'd asked her to come out to the cemetery. To talk. On neutral ground, as it were. We were alone. She hardly struggled beneath the plastic bag marked Armani that I pulled over her head, pulled on the strings. The hard part was feeding her into one of the tubes. I tried to treat her like just another corpse. Like the dead rats I'd had to dispose of when my uni experiments had failed. But this was no experiment and the rest was easy. It was in my field of expertise. I slipped Dr P. into a ceremony with another deceased lined up for cremation. Just some extra ashes. For me, Annette wasn't dead, really. It wasn't her photo on the cylinder. It was somebody else, a spare photo of sorts. I had Annette's photo at home. I had it with me now.

"I never stopped loving you," I said and clinked the cubes in my whisky. "Now you'll always be with me." I kissed her flat black and white face. "Dr Annette Parsons, I've made you immortal." Tomorrow I'll throw out her shoes.

.

A HOME IS A HOME

Harald Sacher knew that help might not come in time. He'd had a good life. Flashes of Margaret in Salzburg faded into others of Edith in Vienna. Edith had been a good wife. So dependable, so tolerant. Yes, he could go easy now, just one last thing, he thought. "Don't forget Valentine's Day," he whispered.

Tears came to Edith's eyes. "I won't," she said and with a gentle motion of her hand she closed his lids forever. She sat a while quietly by his side, holding his still warm hand before going to the living room to call the doctor.

"His heart. Yes, doctor. It was very sudden." Edith kept her voice calm. "No, there's no need to rush now." She did not believe in showing emotions; they were private, like her life, like Harald's. She thought she would have felt more sorrow—it would come of course. But it was just as if he were asleep—or away.

She plumped up the striped silk cushions that sat in the corners of the deep rectangular sofa with its high back and ends supported on straight legs. *Biedermeier.* That was the way Harald liked it. She had to admit, so did she. There were other pieces, too. The writing table for doing the bills and letters, nothing gilt, mind you, just an intimate middle-class style from a bygone age. Why, Harald had even wallpapered the room himself in the same pale green and white stripes of the silk upholstery on the sofa. She'd made the plain Bordeaux velvet curtains which the ceiling-to-wall mirror reflected in a comfortable glow. She had to admit, that he had been right when he'd said that the reticence of decoration was perfectly adapted to the modest size of their flat.

It was this glow that didn't make it so bad when Harald was away all week. His job in the antique business kept him away save for weekends and the odd few days in the month. He was always on the lookout for a new piece. Mostly, he had to...well, it was almost cosset...refurbish pieces in the Salzburg branch. After all, he did have to see things were going well there and he couldn't do that by phone from Vienna.

And they always did go well there. When Harald came home every Friday evening, he glowed with the happiness of one returning to a beloved home.

"A drink, darling?" Edith said as he stretched out on the sofa in his slippers and the smart velvet dressing gown that made him look like Henry Higgins in My Fair Lady.

"Thank you, my dear," he said and brushed her hand with a kiss as she gave him a crystal glass of dark red wine. "I think I'll make a prawn curry tomorrow. I picked up a lovely mixture this week. We shall go to the fish market first thing in the morning."

"Yes, darling, "Edith said as she settled beside him on the sofa. What a boon he was, she thought. A man who loved to cook. Her weekends were always a delight, making up for the empty week in so many ways.

Oh, it wasn't just the sex, the way he'd come back refreshed each weekend. She giggled. It was as if she were his mistress—in a way. No, it was more than that. It was the homey things they did together. The evening drinks, the reading aloud from his favourite books. Lately he'd been reading her Simmel's *Es muß nicht immer Kaviar sein*. She sometimes wondered whether it was the thrill of undercover or the sprinkling of recipes that he enjoyed more. Then there were the trips to the market and the way he waited on her with his superb cuisine. When he left on Monday mornings, he always sealed the comfort of the weekend passed with a tender kiss.

People wouldn't understand, Edith thought, but she couldn't imagine a more comfortable marriage. Why, she even had begun to enjoy the weekdays to herself. She had all the time in the world for her housework and still more to stroll the shops and meet with her friends in the inner-city tea rooms. Yes, indeed, she would miss her husband of thirty years.

Margaret Masoch plumped up the cushions on the pale green and white silk upholstered sofa. As she went to the kitchen to get her cup of tea, she caught sight of her reflection in the mirror that reached from floor to ceiling. "Not bad for 55," she thought and with her forefinger wiped an imaginary blot of lipstick from the corner of her mouth.

It was 10 o'clock on Monday morning. This wasn't like Harald. He always breezed in on the dot of 9:30. He would plant a kiss on her forehead and sit down for a cup of tea with her before they left for the antique shop downtown.

Having him all week somehow made up for the weekends without him. She had her girlfriends, her theatre, her outings to fill them. Sometimes she did find the weekends all too hectic and longed for the comfort and peace of the week.

"A drink, darling," she'd say as he slipped on his dressing gown and slippers. A real gentleman, she thought. They don't come like that anymore these days. Each evening she would try out new dishes. He always enjoyed them, repaying her with compliments and gentle charm.

"The prawn curry is delicious, Margaret. You have surpassed yourself," he had said the week before. "You do spoil me you know."

"But, Harald, I love to spoil you. I love having you to fuss over—it's like having a husband in the home—even after all these years."

Oh, it wasn't just the sex. Not at their age. It was the comfortable evenings after a delicious meal. He would help her put the things away in the kitchen and then they would have a cup of tea and talk about their passion—antique furniture, the speciality—*Biedermeier*. What more could a mistress dream of? Of course, people wouldn't understand; but that was her life, her private life—and his. It was close to 10:30 when the telephone rang.

"Margaret, it's Edith."

Margaret stroked her skirt flat over her thighs. "Yes, Edith. What is it?"

"Harald's dead. His heart.... Are you there, Margaret?"

"Yes, Edith. I'm so sorry."

"So am I, dear. There'll still be the roses for Valentine's Day, though."

.

THE HOG'S BREATH CAFE

Albert Mueller stared at the hand-painted sign on the door of the little pink house.

Gone fishing.

The house was Mardy's haven and was tucked in a corner of the courtyard behind the main three-storey house he had just finished renovating as their permanent home. The little pink house had been his gift to his wife and his way of keeping her, he thought, within the confines of the grounds. Five large garden gnomes huddled by the front door.

Gone pigging, more like it. Albert scowled. She was at it again. Even the haven and the gnomes—one held a pen in its hand—he hadn't been able to find any muses—couldn't make her completely forget Down Under.

Gone fishing. "Just a joke," Mardy had said. "There aren't any fish in the side stream of the Danube." Mardy had other jokes—like the yellow and black sign she tacked on the rear window of her car: Don't follow me, I'm lost, too.

She was lost all right. Lost in her books. And he'd thought the pink haven, the added value that had clinched the house deal, would keep her put. He'd thought that in Vienna she'd have the distance she needed to write.

But he hadn't reckoned with Mardy's need to wander the town, get out and talk to anyone showing the slightest sign of being receptive. He'd thought those days were now over. She could write it all up in her little pink house. But no. She goes fishing. Albert patted the gnome with the pen and went back to the main house and up to their apartments on the first floor. He poured himself a double whisky and stood by the window and gazes down at the lime tree-lined street below.

Ding-dong. The intercom chimed. She'd forgotten her key. He went to the door, pressed the button, and listened for his wife's steps on the marble stairs.

"I'm back," Mardy said. Her hair curled electric about her flushed face. "Guess what. There's a Hog's Breath Café two streets away. They've got kangaroo and wombat signs on the loos."

Albert said nothing.

She giggled. "Roos for the blokes, wombats for the girls."

Albert went back to the window and set his glass down on the sill. "Better tell the gnomes, then."

Mardy came towards him, her eyebrows raised.

"They thought you'd gone fishing."

She slipped her arms around her husband's waist. "There aren't any fish in the Danube anymore," she murmured.

"And pigs?"

"Just memories," she said and pressed herself closer. "The gnomes really do help."

"Mardy."

"I love you, too."

.

PASSIFLORA

I remember when we buried Dad in the back yard. I grated a trough around the tall stump of the liquid amber Mum managed to poison before it fell down on the house in one of those electric storms we get every year. Mum stood wiping her hands on her apron. Watched me. Said nothing.

I'd asked her to wait till I got there. I'd asked him, too, but bloody minded as he'd always been—I'm the one to decide. Respect, and all that. No. It wasn't like that, although I'd preferred it. His marbles just dribbled away like the dregs of his terminal tea until he was spent. Gone.

I sprinkled sweet pea seeds into the trough and then shook out his ashes from the plastic box the crematorium had sent. The box was heavy, the ashes soft. Off-white. My hands trembled as I shook, trying to keep the trough neat. There was enough to go full circle around the 50-year old trunk. I shovelled the mounds and patted the ground down.

His women stood holding hands. Good-bye Dad. Good-bye Dad. I had to go.

Mum, let me know when the sweet peas bloom. Take a photo. And when they shrivel in the heat and floods flash the soil just wait a while, not too long though, and plant something else. Passion fruit, perhaps? And if you have time, forget the cellulose. Capture it in oils. Will you? Please?

WANT OF A STRONG MAN

Ruth had tried not to laugh that day when Anna was sixteen. It would have been fatal since her mouth had been full of pins as she worked on the velvet patchwork bell bottoms for which her grand-daughter had begged.

"I shall never get married," Anna had said. "I shall have lovers. But I shall not marry!"

Slowly Ruth took each pin from her lips. "You may change your mind. 'Never' is one of those words that struggle with time; it's a bit like 'forever'," she had said.

And now, only five years later, Anna, the bride, would, in a few minutes, walk down the aisle on her father's arm.

Ruth smoothed the mauve crepe de chine that covered her knees and let her eyes wander around the old church. It was small. Cool. Simple. A marble altar. The sort of church Martin Luther would have wanted to preach in, the sort of church in which she should have married.

Heinrich would have married her in a church like this. He was the man whose arms had held her, the man who forever would have protected her. But Heinrich was dead. Of a broken neck. Broken necks cannot heal. Not like hearts. Ruth's hand floated to her chest and she closed her eyes to let her fingers feel her heartbeat. A bypass had left its mark, but no one had ever really seen the scar. Albert had noticed it, of course, but for him it had only ever been the proof that everything inside was all right.

Albert was still by her side. The old man sat slightly stooped and stroked his knees with his large fingers. Ruth took his left hand. She traced the swollen veins on its back, the wedding ring glinting against the papery skin of his finger. He had never been a strong man. But he had always been there and now she just had to carry him a little more.

Ruth had always wanted a strong man, but already on her honeymoon she had known that Albert was not the strong man she wanted. She had been lucky to have had a honeymoon at all. It had been wartime then and every year after that, for some reason, there had been no going back.

Not that she hadn't thought of going back. Going back to the homeland. Grabbing her child. Dragging Celia through the brambles growing over the side door of the garage, their first home in Australia, in the Blue Mountains, in Mount Victoria.

Ruth turned her head at the gentle swish of taffeta. A tall, bearded man in morning suit strode proudly past her.

On his arm, Anna, his daughter, her grand-daughter. Anna in cream taffeta.

The priest suddenly stepped out from behind a statue of Saint Christopher. Ruth hadn't noticed the statue at first. She remembered the beard and the staff and the child on the large man's shoulders from a bronze amulet nailed to the dashboard of a car. A bright red car. A sports car. No. This would not have been the right church for Martin Luther after all. Martin Luther never had had his place in this country, her country now, one in which Albert had long since been converted to quiet rambling walks in the bush.

The priest spoke. He welcomed the congregation assembled to celebrate the union of Anna and Alan who faced them, their backs to the altar. The priest was all in white, just the cuffs of his jeans peeped out from beneath his robes, Ruth noticed. So different from her own wedding, she thought.

She had stood with Albert before the mayor whose shirt tail saluted stiffly through his unbuttoned fly. They'd got the mayor out of bed at two in the morning. Albert had been due to leave for the front. Things had to go quickly in 1942.

Dear Albert, Ruth thought and gripped the old man's hand. Who would have thought that they'd see the millennium, and now it had come like any of the other passing years? Albert was a good man; but with each year he had leaned on her more and more. And all she had ever wanted was her one strong man.

Anna's father. Rob. Now, Rob was a strong man, Ruth thought and looked across at her daughter, Anna's mother, sitting on the other side of the church. Celia did not look her age. None of the women of the family did. Ruth smiled at the thought. Celia had done her own thing. She had run off with Rob. Las Vegas. Just a telegram. We got married today. Love. Celia had married her strong man. But where had it got her? Celia was happy. Yes, Ruth thought. Celia was happy. She would have had more lines, more grey hairs, had she been less so. Ruth brushed her forehead with her hand as if trying to brush away a cobweb. Celia was a writer. Writers.

They wanted everything, but were never fulfilled. They were always traipsing off after their characters, as if they were lovers, Ruth suddenly thought. Funny that she should think of them as lovers. Surely there were other important characters in Celia's head. Ones more important than lovers. Ruth remembered that there had been times when she had been seriously worried about the state of her daughter's mental health. Was it possible to cram all those people into one head? All at the same time? No. Celia could not be fulfilled. Even if Rob was a strong man. It was not his fault. And Celia had not been a writer back in Las Vegas. That had only come later.

How many generations did it take, Ruth wondered, to find out that love was not what one thought it would be. Rob did not seem to mind, she thought as she looked at his beard. A wife other than Celia would insist it be clipped. But this is Anna's wedding, not Celia's, Ruth said to herself and straightened up against the wooden backrest.

The young man, the groom,—his name was Alan—stood stiffly with his back to the altar. Ruth was sure that he'd swayed just a fraction towards his bride before straightening up and wiping his right hand over the wool of his black knife-creased trousers. Anna stood tall and serene by his side. She resembles a lily, Ruth thought. It was the first time Ruth had seen her granddaughter with anything less than a freesia blush since she had rushed in that day just three months ago to introduce the young man who had brought her home in the red sports car.

"This is Alan, Gran," Anna had said, as if she had just caught the impossible fish that was always much longer and stronger than its own waters of reality would allow.

Later, out on the porch, swinging on the couch alone with her grand-daughter, Ruth had asked: "And what about all those lovers?"

"Oh, Gran," Anna had said. "You only say that when you haven't got any." Anna leaned over, stretched out her legs and placed her head in Ruth's lap. "I'm so much in love. Just like you were. Just like you were, like you still are, with Grandpa."

Ruth's hand stroked her grand-daughter's blonde hair back from her brow. "I know what you mean," she said. "I know what you're asking." Anna closed her eyes and Ruth kept on stroking. "How can anyone know if it's all," she heard herself whisper.

The priest turned to face the congregation. Ruth squeezed Albert's hand. A tiny smile flickered beneath his white moustache. Anna's father, looking more and more like the patron saint of voyagers, settled in by his wife's side. Ruth watched as he held a white handkerchief for his wife to take. Celia had been so lucky, she thought. And she hardly knew it. Ruth watched her daughter wipe the corner of her eye with the handkerchief. A movement of Rob's arm told her that he had received the bunched up cloth for stowing into his pocket. Ruth sighed. Celia had never wanted to hang onto soggy hankies. Ruth closed her eyes for a second. What if? What if, only Heinrich? She shook her head. There would have been no Celia. There would have been no Anna. But she would have perhaps known what Anna might know, what even, her daughter, Celia had perhaps once known. Suddenly an arrythm fluttered and Ruth's hand went to her heart. Now it was far too late for all that. She had at least had her Heinrich. Ruth took a deep breath. Her pulse was beginning to calm. She leant forward to listen. The moment had come.

The priest was asking the one question that could make the voice of the strongest man quaver. "Do you?" the question that demanded just one two-word answer. Ruth watched as Alan gripped Anna's hand. When she married Albert, she'd been asked first. Times had changed, she thought. Or had they really? She shook her head as if to brush away the thought. Ruth fixed her eyes on Alain. He did not fluff his lines. "I do." How easy, Ruth thought. How easy for him to commit for a lifetime.

The priest then turned to Anna and asked the same question. Ruth felt a stillness about her, like smoke hung in the air after fireworks. A murmur rose through the pews.

As Anna's eyes met hers Ruth took Albert's hand. The fingers of her other hand began to tremour, only coming to rest in the dying echo of her granddaughter's "Yes!"

STILETTO CONDOMS

A little kinky.

Me?

And you're ruining everything.

I thought you liked it.

I do.

Who's kinky now?

Just touch.

He took her hand and guided it over the parquet floor. "It cost me a fortune," he said.

"Very nice."

"But can you feel them?"

"Them?"

"The pock marks. Pock marks all over it."

"Interesting."

"You know how that happened?"

"How?"

He glanced sideways at her stilettos on the floor.

"But I thought you liked them."

"I do."

"And you always ask me to take off my clothes."

"I do?"

She ran a hand over his clavicle. "You always say, take them off."

"I do," he said.

She'd come in the door and he'd tell her to take them off. She'd unbutton her blouse and slip out of her skirt and then, stark naked but for the stilettos, she'd come towards him and, and well, who could say no? His parquet, though, was showing the strain.

The parquet is suffering.

The parquet?

Your stilettos.

She ran her fingers over the pock marks on the floor. "Is it me or the parquet thing?"

She didn't come for a whole week. He rang. "I'm busy," she said.

"I miss you."

"And the parquet?"

"I love you," he said.

"In stilettos?"

"Yes."

"And the parquet?"

"More pock marks, I guess."

He opened the door. "Take them off," he said. "Your clothes, I mean."

Smiling, she placed two woolly thinglets into his hand and proceeded to undress.

He slipped one of the thinglets over a finger, the other over a thumb. Naked, she lifted one stiletto-clad foot. "Slip it on," she said.

He smiled.

"Now the other."

"I love you," he said as his eyes ran approvingly over her body down to her felt-clad stiletto heels.

"Condoms," she said. "For the parquet."

TOCK-TOCKING

They made me take off my bra and the gold chain round my neck. It had been my grandfather's and used to be linked to the fob attesting to the passing of time. He died before the war could get him. My grandmother died of cancer as did her son, my uncle. Dad hung in there until the pacemaker batteries died. Mum's willing herself away.

As the tunnel closed over me and the tock-tocking dulled my senses I figured I'd had a good run for my money. I'd seen the world, known love, never lost it, shared my life and my words. I was at peace with myself for those few minutes. I get the same feeling every time I take off in a plane. Then I forget.

But it's different now. How much time is left to do all the things I must do? An essay to finish. What madness made me commit to such research? But commit is commit. All the sins know that. Do I need to revise them? Leave them part of the story. A novel. Almost there. At least I'll be saved the rejections. Maybe I'll have time to be there for

Mum. And to see our daughter's graduation. But there are so many papers to go through, mess to clean up, arrangements to make. And there's the dog.

I've put the gold chain back on. It just links to itself. No interfering fob any more. Time is today. Every moment. Move on. Regrets? Not really. In fact, none at all. Not even the smoking, but I'm glad our daughter doesn't. Maybe I put her off. Maybe I saved her life, for a while at least. The chain gleams in my fingers in the way of old gold. Tonight, I'll be getting back the results.

CHRISTMAS GOOSE

Christmas and fat geese. Fat. Goose. What a goose I was to think that Christmas would fix everything. Time of cheer. Family. Peace. Home. I was out of it. On the other side of the world in the middle of an argument with the love of my life. Skype kept cutting off. Email. He doesn't answer emails, just reads them. I could hardly post 'Luv U' on my blog, and texting was out of the question for the love of my life had three thumbs. There was more of me, too.

Weeks passed and I pined. I had to see him. Bring him a gift. Both meant money I didn't have. Passion makes possible, I chanted. I ate only salads, drank only water, walked and jogged everywhere I went. Sometimes I was even faster than the bus, but only when it was going the other way. In the Op Shop I bought five metres of red ribbon and asked the butcher for ten sheets of wrapping paper, promising to pick the turkey up later. My old car was getting lonely, I know, as I wasn't driving it any more. Bye, Morris, I said. I have to sell you.

I bought a cheap ticket via Beijing and Virgin and landed shivering in the snow. With my paper and ribbon under my arm, I hitched a ride to town. Then I wrapped myself up in the paper and rolled about in the metres of ribbon. I tied a bow around my middle and another around my forehead. People were hurrying home. The smell of mulled wine was in the air. Candles glowed from behind windows. I rang his bell. The door opened. "Merry Christmas," I said.

He pulled me inside, kissing me around the bows. "I knew it was you," he said.

THE MEMORY BOX

Jewellery can be just a work of art. Did I say just? No. If it's design, it needs to have some practical purpose. But your practicality, she thought, is perhaps my serendipity. That had always been the way with him and he never gave up. But all that was now in the past, and she was firmly in the present with a project to complete.

It's not just rings on your fingers and bells round your neck, she thought as she took two pieces of aluminium. She cut and filed tiny leaf holes all over them until her fingers and thumbs were coated in silvery dust; here and there thin scratches stopped just short of blood. She shaped the two pieces into the form of praying hands: not ones that were pressed together, those that let life still breathe in.

The silvery grey of the metal was cold, so she enamelled the pieces in ruby red. She dried them on their backs like open palms, and then on their fronts, humped like twin turtles.

She took his love letter and ripped it into scraps. The tears lacerated the words "I", "love" and "you". There were so many of them. She piled them into one of the halves and quickly trapped them with the other. With a thin white silk ribbon she laced the two humps of her life together. She wanted to tie a long flowing bow, but the ribbon was too short. There was only enough for a tight little knot.

The humps now resembled a heart: not the Valentine sort, the one shaped like a fist. She cupped it in both hands and shook it about. The love scraps danced and whichever way she stopped the three little words peeked out at her from within her memory box.

UNCLE HENRI

Everyone in the village was talking about the man who'd asked the little girl to accompany him to the park. Then someone overheard Henri say: "Come with me." And they'd seen the little girl hesitate and then put her hand in his. They'd watched him go down the street and round the corner and when he was out of sight, they still saw him, hand in hand with the little blonde girl. They saw him lead her over behind the garden house in the far corner of the park and they saw him bend down, stroke her hair, unbutton her coat, untie her shoelaces. And it all became too much. So they called the police.

Henri yelled and the little girl screamed. Someone took her aside as they dragged him away. That was the last she saw of him. When he got out a few months later, he shot himself.

The little girl is grown up now. She sits and stares at old photos of her uncle Henri. She still blames herself for that day in the park. That blame has followed all her growing up. She couldn´t understand then, not even now, what all the fuss was about. Shortly after they took Henri away, she´d noticed how her godfather, even her own father, wouldn´t pick her up or hug her when other people were around. It was as if that sort of thing was suddenly forbidden, forever. She wanted hugs from those she loved, wanted the world to see.

Today she finds it hard to make contact. She fears that once she makes it, they'll take it away, like they took away her uncle Henri. They´d skirted the garden house, he´d pushed her so high on her favourite swing. It had been the last happy day of her life.

THE HALO

I was sitting in my office waiting for the phone to ring. It hadn´t rung for a while, but I was a patient man. That was my business. Being patient. Then at the slightest whiff of something off, nosing in to sniff things out. My speciality was divorce. But with all the counselling couples were now taking up like a sport, my forte was as strong as lavender in a pot of steaming tar. No match. I was scraping under my fingernails with the letter opener when the phone rang and I almost dropped the receiver.

"Do you do thefts?" a woman´s voice said, lisping the last word.

"Lady, I´m a private eye. You need the police." I was about to slam the phone down and go back to my nails, when she said. "Wait!"

It wasn´t just the urgency of her voice that kept me connected, it was a certain timbre with husky Lauren Bacall feel to it. I could just see her. Redhead. Had to be.

I leant back in my swivel chair and tipped my hat into my eyes. "What's your problem, lady?" I drawled and then heard her sigh.

"I've been robbed."

"Police?" I had the feeling we´d been there before.

"They´ll think I'm crazy."

"Maybe I will, too."

"Please."

"Shoot, lady."

What she said next sounded like "halo".

"Your what?" But business was business. Nutters also got into trouble. Maybe it was code. "Someone pinch it off your head?" Geez, I hoped she had money. My time wasn´t free. "Lady. Hope you can pay. If you can't, I'll have to hang up. I'm a busy man." Yeah. Nails were waiting.

"I´m sorry," she said. "Of course I can pay. But you have to believe me." There was a pause. "How did you know?" she said.

TRASHION PASSION

She recycled him. Right from the first question: "Got any old jumpers?"

"They're for the needy," he said.

She looked out at him from under her fringe. "They're fashion conscious, too. Give me what they wouldn't want."

"Anything?"

He gave her his teabags and ties, old jeans, zippers and ski gloves.

"More," she said, and so he set off to ask all his friends.

"Why?" they asked.

"She needs them," he said.

They shook their heads.

"All this enough now?" he asked with arms laden.

She nodded and arranged piles on the floor.

"Why?" he said softly.

She winked, shook her head, just said: "Wait and see."

She worked for hours on end, days and weeks, and all the while he sat cross-legged and watched her.

She frilled all his ties and sewed them together and made them into a long shiny skirt.

"You'll need a bodice," he said, his eyes caressing her breasts. "Better still. We could stay here forever."

She blew him a kiss and arranged all the tea bags, strings hanging down like Swarovski pendants.

"A necklace perhaps?"

She blew him a prfft! And proceeded to triangulate all her zippers until she had a collar like *Comme des Garcons*.

"What if I take you walking in the snow?"

"Can't catch me," she said and slipped her legs into faded legwarmers that covered her Moon Boots and were made from his jeans.

"But your shoulders. It's cold outside."

She gestured to him that he remain seated while she arranged hundreds of ski gloves in a pattern over old jumpers. She sewed and she stitched hands, wrists and fingers until a cuddle-warm cape was completed.

He clapped his hands. "My princess," he said.

"Trash is my passion," she said proudly.

He held out his arms. "My trashion is you."

FLOATING

She couldn't really swim, but she knew that if she lay back straight and breathed deeply she might be able to float. So she dipped her big toe into the wild waters of the web, jiggled it about and then jumped in. She went under at first, but when she spat out mouthfuls of sherbet water she soon found that it wasn't as deep as she'd feared. So she went with the flow and let herself be washed ashore to a place where words played with each other.

They came from all sides and the strangest of places. Some were in code masquerading as numbers. Others spoke of giraffes and dragons, and also of love: love found, love lost, love in waiting, love wanting. Words jostled and danced in groups of 300, playing with line breaks and colons and dashes. The stories they sang touched all generations and flew off and about, touching new places: gut, heart, geography and mind. There was food there, too: chocolate and fish, cups of tea, coffee and wine, even magic mushrooms and smoking signs. Odd names would flit past, some even with faces. Others wore pictures coded in colours.

Words washed over her, shook and cajoled her; some started teaching her how to swim. Lift your arm, breathe deep, flap your feet, play like a dolphin, but mind the sharks and the obscure fish. Don't worry about what's going on at the homestead. Play with us now, come on now. Swim. So she stroked and flapped, but as she turned over, she heard a voice say: "Come home now, we need you." She turned back and saw a big wave coming, so duty bound surfed back to the shore.

"Where've you been now?" asked her husband.

"Floating, just floating," she said with a grin.

MARZIPAN DREAMS

From the moment he saw her looking down through the glass panes into the kitchen, he couldn't get her out of his mind. He usually took no notice of the people milling up and down the stairs that led to the rooms where coffee and pastries were served. He knew he was on show; the pastry cooks always were at Demel's. When in Vienna, one went there for the best pastries in the world. It was probably Schnitzler's fault that the old coffee house exploited a touch of Blue Room voyeurism.

On the way down from the first-floor rooms, although you had to keep moving, you could see through the glass how the marzipan was rolled. Finished products were displayed in a vitrine at the entrance: the mini ex-Chancellor waltzing with his tall blonde Minister of Foreign Affairs; Tina Turner; Bill Clinton.

A pause in the movement on the stairs caught his eye. She'd stopped the traffic. She was staring at his fingers rolling the mixture of fine almonds and sugar. He felt her gaze caress them as he kneaded. He added a drop of rum to the mixture and felt a look in her eyes silk over his cheeks. He blushed, kept on kneading. Then his fingers began to move more quickly as he rolled and tweaked the thick fragrant paste. Sensing a movement, he looked up from his ministrations. The figures on the stairs again had taken up their perpetual motion, blurring the pause that she had been.

With new fervour his fingers began sculpting the marzipan mass. He wanted no colourants. Wanted it natural. Although he couldn't be sure if she'd ever know how he felt, he piped a thin stream of chocolate onto a white ice-sugar label: Reclining Nude. Maybe she'd see it in the vitrine.

ALBANIAN COGNAC

He didn't go off with the others to the *Gasthaus*.

"Why not?" I asked.

"I'm *Tschusch*," he said.

I was familiar with the derogatory expression the Viennese used for anyone that came from the East of their border. They couldn't always tell, of course, so it was sometimes used when someone spoke funny. I'd even been called that myself when I tried to get my tongue around the local accent.

"Me too," I said.

"Nah."

"S'truth."

He'd come from what was now Kosovo. Had worked hard and drew a small pension he rounded off by helping out with the dirty work.

"*Tschusch* work," he said. "You don't do that."

"Aren't you hungry?" I asked.

"Maybe some sandwiches? I can pay."

I cut some black bread and spread butter, then I added three types of sausage. He'd worked hard on the house. I wanted to do it. "No pork," I said. "It's all turkey clone."

"I don't mind sausage," he said.

"Aren't you Muslim?"

He shrugged. "I like salami."

"And wine? Want a *Spritzer*?"

"Just water."

We sat on the bench and he told me about when the Russians had come and he'd lost everything. He'd started again. Nineteen cows, a house. Then came the cleansing. "I've got nothing left to lose," he said.

When the fires raged through and water became scarce, he started to cry.

"I have to go home," he said. "Just for a week. See how things are."

On the day he left he'd had a haircut and clipped his eyebrows. I gave him some cuttings from the garden. "Their roots are soaked; they should last the bus ride."

Last week he came by and pressed a small bottle into my hand. "Albanian cognac," he said. "Made the same way, in the same place, for 500 years."

IMAGINATION

She'd known him for ages, through work, as it was with all the men that she knew. They'd always got on, talked shop and joked, and ignored any frisson they might have felt. Then they lost touch, at least for a while.

"I'm coming for work," she said on the phone.

"I'll pick you up."

"Take me to my hotel?"

She stood at the counter while he held her case. "Just one night," she said to the man at reception.

"A double room, Ma'am?" the clerk said with what she felt was the slightest of smirks.

"Single," she said.

"Then twin beds," the clerk answered in statement of fact.

She shrugged.

She poured him a drink as he sat on one bed. She reached him his glass and sat down on the other. He raised it and smiled. She hesitated. She thought she'd imagined the back of his hand fleet over her breast as she sat down. She shook her head slowly. "Cheers," she said.

"I can't stay long," he said. "My wife …"

"You didn't tell her?"

He shook his head.

"Never shop talk?"

He nodded.

She thought he looked sad, just for an instant. Or maybe she was imagining that, too.

"How long are you staying?"

"Just the night," she said.

"Will you ring me before you leave?"

She nodded.

"I'd better go now," he said and drained his glass. "Have a good meeting. It was good seeing you."

Good seeing you, too, she thought.

She watched him walk down the hall, saw him turn, give a wave. She raised her hand limply, and the door shut behind him.

The next day at checkout she phoned as promised. "It was good," she said.

There was a silence at his end. She waited.

"You didn't imagine it," he said.

SWEET DREAMS

Dreams are funny things. You go to bed and snuggle under your doona and think you're at peace with the world. Before you know it you're walking down High Street, right foot on the kerb, left in the gutter. Wait a minute. It's not you at all. This is my dream.

Men and women dressed in warm coats and boots, their faces muffled in scarves and caps, walked past me, staring and pointing. I looked around and saw they meant me. No one said a word. The foot in the gutter kept getting stuck in a shiny brown mass. I grabbed hold of my knee and yanked the foot up. Then I saw my reflection in a shop window. I was naked except for goose pimples all over my body and toffee enclosing my left foot like a boot.

I suppose it was the toffee that did it. I'd been melting butter and dribbling in sugar, spinning it around in a frying pan. It wasn't the toffee I was after; it was a smell I'd been trying to retrieve. I wanted to breathe in that carefree time of marshmallows and apples. Go back to when people's stares didn't matter. When nobody fired sticks and stones. When nobody cared if I played in the gutter. All that came later, when I grew up.

In my dream, the goose pimples felt like a cloak. I wasn't cold and I wasn't scared. The only thing strange was that sticky toffee.

When I woke up my body felt warm, but my ankles were icy. I pulled back the doona and rubbed my feet. My sheet was speckled with crumbles of toffee. I sighed and reached for the tweezers that I keep on my night table and picked out the slivers from between my toes.

GARLI VON CLOVE

I hate *fondue*! Hey! We're talking cheese here—*Vacherin* of the cow, and *Gruyère* from the mountain—a real thick cheesy mess. Everyone wants it, and it'll be the end of me.

Has anyone ever thought of me? Me, that's Garli von Clove. OK, I don't get dropped into clarified butter to sizzle to a dark shade of done, and I don't get smothered in thick melting chocolate—but you never know, that might happen one day, the way folks are playing about with their taste buds. But let's get back to now and the plunging barometer, the Fondue season's open.

Fondue! Fondue! They scream. And for me that means that I'll be pulled from my mates and my coat will get peeled off and I'll be left shivering naked on the kitchen sink. Ever seen grown men sipping at *Chasselas* and grating and grating at great hunks of cheese? Big yellow and beige chunks end up as just so much of a mound of gratings. And I'm shivering, but now it's for fear.

Fat fingers squeeze me and push me flat against the side of a big bowl. Hey! That's cold! And before I can say anything else off we go. Around and around and up and down. I'm getting dizzy. Hey! I've been over that bit before. I'm feeling very squashed now. I'm a Von not a *Fon*! Don't do that to me!

I'm all squelched out, but at least I can rest, and no one can see me. Oh, no! I try and pull what's left of my head in. Here it comes! I'm drowning. It's getting hot. I hang onto the edge of a wooden spoon swaying about in a creamy sea. It's getting thicker and hotter. Schwish! He doused me, mmmm, with,…hic! Mmmm. Nice. Cool. Wine. Yep. White wine. And off we go again. Now that spoon's speeding up. Swoosh! Whoops! Ha! That was good! Strong! Yeah! Hickety-hic! Tastes of Kirsch? Yeah, I could get used to…hic!…to this. Think I'll stretch out. Round and round. Slowing down. Getting sleepy.

Oh, no! He's skewering me with a ball of bread. I'll hang onto those strings of elastic cheese—he's pulling and twirling, I'm getting dizzy. I'm gonna fall off! No! Not the whiskers. He's already trapped cheese strings in his handlebar moustache. I'm going, going, going. Gulp. Gone.

CHICLE ALERT

I can't tell a cliché from a *chicle*, except that the latter is Mexican. I can chew on them both for countless hours, which probably explains why I like Ferdinand. So let me take the bull by the horns all the way to China. I tend to jump out of the frying pan, so here's my bull story.

Ferdinand is an alpha bull. He loves to smell flowers and is gentle and sweet. One day, he got hit by anosmia and couldn't smell anything anymore. But he remembered how his horse friends would nibble the flowers he'd get his nose into, and he loved horses nearly as much. That's why I took him to China. It was tough getting him on the plane to Xi'an, but I dressed him in a pink coat and we went economy with Virgin. They're not too fussy and even said we could fly to Mars with them once the route was up. But we had China in our sights now. Ferdinand had always wanted to see Emperor Quin's terracotta army, not so much for the soldiers, but for the horses. He was very gentle and didn't break a thing. Told you he was alpha.

On the way back we detoured over Mexico. Ferdinand wanted some of that gum. I'd told him that we had *Chiclets* at home, but he wanted the real thing. Before I knew it he'd swallowed a whole 500gm serving and was well into chewing his cud by the time we landed. He burped his way through immigration and at the scan desk a huge blob of gum in his belly came up. *Chicle* alert!

Seems *Chiclets* are on the soon-to-be- banned list and Ferdinand copped it for smuggling the stuff. They took him away and it broke my bleeding heart.

JUNGLE GREENS

He's strutting down the main drag carrying a black attaché case to match his high heels and stockings. His legs and chest are unshaved. His jungle-green bra matches his suspender belt and panties. Nobody looks at him. They're not even averting their eyes. They just don't notice.

My husband dreams in media res, in colours and scenes and wakes up in a sweat before any epiphany. That's when I say, tell me, and he does.

"Can I have it?" I say.

"You're so greedy."

"Ha!"

"What do you do with them all?"

I grin.

"I don't want to know," he says.

There's the one when I gave him a glass with a hairline crack and red wine seeped over his new white shirt. There's another where the tiles in the kitchen were falling off the wall, and when he tried to catch them, they just fell more quickly. Once he's given me his dreams, he forgets them, he says.

I don't analyse his dreams, I just play with them. I can sit for hours doodling and moodling.

"I don't want to go there," he says.

"Where?"

"Into that head of yours."

"It's no big deal," I say.

"I can hear little cogs creaking away."

"That's because I'm exploring stories."

"I don't want to go there. Not with this last one."

When he was wearing his jungle-green undies, a writing mate had come to stay.

He told her his dream.

"Can I have it?" she said.

"Hey, but it's mine," I said.

He looked at us both and shook his head slowly. "Why don't you just share it?"

My writing mate hasn't done anything with his dream yet, and my little cogs keep skipping past the jungle-green lace.

HAPPY?

Hey, what's this for? The Book of My Face Spice? You already know my name, my age, my sex, my town, my friends; you've got my pic, and my accent. And now you ask me all these happy questions. You fire them at me, triggering a cacophony of smells: warm milk and frankfurters, cinders, doonas, wet stones and slime, and pink marshmallows.

I hear shouts and screams and gentle warbling. Songs and shudders paint the walls.

Einstein's tongue is licking the fine hairs at my nape as we roll with the pigs in the magic of mushrooms. Giggles like bubblegum burst over my face and clog up my nose. I am dying. I am flying. Memories mingle with flowers and brickbats, soaked in aromas of vegemite jam. And there are the dragons, the ones that I fight with. The red ones, the blue ones, the lizards of the land. And the land, it is dry, yet the waters are rising and there's a green goo at the end of the road. Or was that your nose?

Rights, you ask? Who has rights these days? Secure rights? Right to security? I hear the gallop of oxen and morons. Of course I cry, and I'm not ashamed. I sometimes do it so much that I pee. Maybe that's where it lives, in a five n' ten bladder.

I ask myself many things, but don't often get answers. I should be so lucky, but let's not moot the point. You still with me? It's whiskers on raindrops, and brown-paper geese and all of that's hard to sew as a costume. But it tastes of sherbet. And it fizzes on your tongue and warms the skin on your wishbone.

You think you've got my number, but you forgot to ask if I were happy.

THE PACKAGE

"I'll take the package," I said. They could have been famous last words before it all blew up in my face. Trouble was, he wasn't listening, or if he was, he couldn't hear me. My voice had got stuck somewhere between my heart and my epiglottis.

The package had been my dream. The way out of the day job. A now or never deal.

"Speak up."

I choked.

"Too bad," he said.

I stared at him with my mouth open, but no words came out. It was all over.

I skulked back to my one-window office, grabbed my bottle of Evian and gargled. Then I spat into the aspidistra. Five more years. A life sentence. I would die.

Hey, why not? Even that would be better than endless Excel charts that fudged the stats. I'd go down, but I'd go down swinging. Maybe even get famous, though I probably wouldn't be around to see it. Vincent had cut off his ear in frustration. I'd go one better.

I found out how to do it on the Web. Wasn't too hard, although I did get my fingers into a bit of a twist with the wiring. I had a brown paper bag. He didn't deserve pretty paper.

I got all dressed up and went to the top floor.

"About that package," I said.

He looked at me over the pile on his desk. "It's too late."

"Yeah, I reckon," I said and held out the bag.

He got up. Then everything went black.

I came to in the ward, hands and ears blown off. They couldn't charge me in that state. Seems that the stats got burned up in the blast, but he got away with just a scratch. I'm on invalidity now. It'll take time, but it changed my life.

DUCK'S DISEASE

I guess Barbie thinks that she's got it all, but I've got it better. I've got duck's disease; my tummy's too close to the ground. The negatives are just from her point of view. My legs are as straight as hers, but my arms are longer. It's in the family. It didn't bother me when I was littler than little. A bit of a bother started at school when all the other girls shot up. And then there were the clothes.

Weekends were OK, because that's when you could wear any old thing, or new, if you had it. But weekdays in that great equalizer, the school uniform, they were the pits. You tell me how you can hitch up your block pleats to show off your knees when your bum's in the way.

There were advantages, though. No plaster casts from basketball falls—you don't fall far when your centre of gravity only has to plumb several inches. It was a hassle getting up on the stools in the chemistry lab, but I loved chemistry. It put us on the same level, and I learnt to follow my nose. You wouldn't believe the stuff you can smell when you're close to the ground. It's a shock at first, but with practice and time you become selective.

First there were flowers—dwarf iris and jonquils and chocolate cosmos—and then there were herbs—thyme, mint and lemon balm. Today I can sniff out a pheromone from a footprint. The shoe's on the other foot now and who cares about *Manolo Blahnik*? I can walk on my hands if I want to wobble and I'm told there's something seductive about the way that I waddle. I don't have to be stuck with any old Ken, the world is my bowl of truffles.

GOLDEN LOVER

"Happy birthday, darling." A breakfast kiss on the cheek and she was forty-one.

Barbara stared at her face in the mirror: Wrinkles? The lines grinned back at her. She didn't really feel different. Exactly one year earlier she'd marvelled that there'd been no dreaded bang. The party helped too. She wiped the bridge of her nose: why do I always manage to smudge the mascara? She shrugged, winked at the laugh lines and went downstairs. The dress rehearsal was over and she knew it.

"See you! I'm off to pick up Damian," she called to her husband still breakfasting in the cosy kitchen.

"All right, dear. I'll clean up in the meantime."

Driving to the station Barbara reflected on her luck. He really does help when it counts. Not bad after twenty years.

The tall young man stood behind the last taxi stand. His blonde hair tumbled over his forehead as his head scouted left then right. She recognised him immediately although it had been ten years since she last had seen him. She dismissed the tiny tug in her chest as the pleasure of seeing the son of her oldest friend again. Barbara had grown up with Damian's mother but time had reduced their friendship to Christmas and birthday cards, revived by infrequent visits.

Barbara pulled in to park in the loading zone behind the taxi stand and left the door of her Honda open as she leapt out and called: "Damian!"

He had noticed the white run-around tear up to park in front of him, but it was only when she called his name that he realised who she was. "Barbara, it's good to see you," he grinned.

"Give me your things-have to hurry or I'll get a ticket-we'll talk in the car."

It was Saturday morning and there was the usual heavy traffic, but Barbara found she had to concentrate more on the road this time.

Damian watched her face as she steered skilfully through the sea of traffic, riding the wave of green lights.

"How was the trip?" Her eyes held the road.

"I slept most of the way. Hardly smelt the snoring feet -the train was full."

Barbara found herself wondering which berth had been his. He must have had his head where the others had their feet. She giggled.

"What's so funny?"

"I'm just imagining you in the middle berth. Snoring feet. I guess they do smell when you're filed away like that."

The car pulled into the drive. John was standing at the front door. "Why Damian, how you've grown. He's grown, hasn't he, Barbara?"

"Yes, indeed he has." She looked him over and found she enjoyed it.

"Hallo, John. You see, I did come, just like I said I would -when I was bigger, just like I said."

Barbara remembered her own exact words ten years earlier: "Yes of course you can, when you're bigger."

"John, why don't you help Damian with his things while I make some tea." The mirror in the hall smiled as she passed.

From the kitchen window she watched the two men as they unloaded the car. They were about the same height, both lanky. They looked like friends.

Barbara was preparing the tea as the men entered the oak-panelled kitchen. She placed a steaming cup on the table in front of Damian and her fingers brushed the air thick between their hands. She caught his eye and felt the tug in her chest again. It made her turn her back to look for a chore, get the sugar, the milk, the lemon.

"Milk or lemon?"

She relaxed as her husband said: "Just a spot of milk, darling."

"Lemon for me, please, Barbara," said Damian, his voice betraying nothing of the secrets his gaze had laid bare.

Standing behind her husband's chair, Barbara placed her hand on John's shoulder. "How are your parents, Damian?"

Damian told them the latest news: the new furniture in the living room, his mother's new-found interest in computers, his father's heavy work schedule. "At least they have work and are busy," John said, "that's half the satisfaction these days."

"What are you going to do, Damian," he asked. Barbara took her hand from John's shoulder and sat down at the table.

"Theatre," said Damian. As if to defend the word, he added: "I've been accepted to do drama. I'm going to be an actor." Barbara remembered his teenage spoofs, his antics and impersonations. He was good. Would it be enough? What did she care? "When do courses start?" Barbara asked.

"Next week. I can only stay the weekend, if you'll have me, that is."

"You can stay as long as you like," Barbara heard her husband say as he left to fetch his pipe.

Barbara took the red and white checked cloth and wiped the table. Through golden lashes streaked with daytime, Damian's eyes followed the movement of her forearm over the table-top. His fingers trapped a hem. She felt the tug and let it pull. They swayed suspended, their only harness red and white.

"Where did I leave my tobacco pouch, Barbara?" John called from the study. "Oh, I've got it. Won't be a minute."

The dish cloth dropped, drowned their magic. Barbara giggled, caught the erring cloth and hung it back onto its hook on the door as if in reprimand. She looked at Damian. His eyes swam in questions.

John sat down at the table, his pipe glowing with the sweet earthy smell of nuts. "We can pop around to the McDonnell's tonight. They have a daughter your age, Damian. You don't want to spend all the time with us oldies, do you?" Barbara sat down at her husband's side.

"If you don't mind I'd rather just stay here," Damian said. "I am a bit tired from the trip, the snoring feet."

"Snoring feet?"

"Yes, John, that's Damian's way of describing the sleep he got in the train last night," Barbara grinned.

"Snoring feet. Not bad. Did they smell that loudly?" The three of them burst out laughing. "Well, we'll stay in if you like, but I'll just pop round to Jim McDonnell's anyway, just for a quick drink."

"John needs to stretch his water wings from time to time; Scotch and water wings, eh John?"

"Now, now, darling, don't make me out to be like that," he said, giving her a light pat on the shoulder and a kiss on the cheek as he stood up. "I won't be long."

Leaning her face upon her elbowed hand, Barbara pushed her cheek into wrinkles. "What is it, Damian?"

"Nothing. Just tired, I guess." He hesitated,

"You're funny. I mean…please don't get mad."

"Go on," she said, freeing her cheek. The fingers of her right hand began teasing her wedding ring.

"I bet you like happy ends. That's when you let yourself go."

Her eyes forced his gaze, but her fingers kept worrying the ring.

"But when you don't know what the end will be like," he pursued. "You just forge ahead, cold as ice."

The tug pulled harder. "I don't follow," she half whispered, knowing she did. It was something to do with half measures, following one's star.

"I'm sorry," he said. "Maybe it's just me. I don't know what to do and you,…you just sit there and smile."

Barbara knew she couldn't just walk away from this strange and disturbing conversation. She reached over and stroked the hair from his eyes. "Poor darling," she said, "you can hear with your nose and your eyes say so much." She didn't know what else to say; she didn't want him to become part of all the well-known clichés.

Isn't it funny, she thought, am I so much more susceptible now than I would have been at the right age? What is the right age, anyway? The feeling in her chest had eased. "Let's go for a walk," she said. He was right, she was forging again.

They strolled around the garden and stopped to sit on the teak bench facing the avenue of poplars that marked the property boundary. The evening sky still held cloudy shapes in its flattened dome. "What can you see up there, Damian? Leaping frogs, sheep?"

He leant his head back and to one side, just grazing her shoulder: "I see imprisoned princes and princesses and I want to block them out." His face turned towards hers. She swam in his eyes, feeling the caress of his golden lashes.

"I'm home," John's voice called from the front gate.

"Round the back," Barbara heard herself echoing.

He came and stood before them, his face to the clouds. "A lovely sky," he said.

Barbara looked up. There was too much at stake, the choice was hers. She saw the cloud games, leaping frogs.

"Yes, it is darling. Indeed it is."

THE FROZEN TEAR

It's never the snow's fault. It's just the way your mind works, maybe more attuned to cold than to heat. It's when you come out and see a frozen tear on your windscreen, one that won't melt in the slithering frost. And then fires rage. And on the other side of the world there's burning and you smell smoke and catch a whiff of eucalyptus. And the flames skip through the treetops and they're so close and you hope and pray that they've cleaned out the guttering on the roof of the house you turned your back on so many years ago.

The house always survived through the years, through the fires. That's what they told you. You believed them. You never thought beyond your big doona coat and keeping yourself warm.

And now you stand in the cold and want to roll up your sleeves, help in some way; and your hand grabs the scraper and guts the soft frost, but the tear doesn't budge. So you go back and fetch a cup of hot water. It's sizzling around you, the flames licking closer. It's been dry for years, and you never noticed. You never noticed the years spin into decades of big warm doonas.

You never noticed the heat. It was warmth that you wanted. But now in the cold it's warmer than comfort. You see hoses trained on the house back home. You want to be there passing the buckets, doing your bit to make the fires go out.

You pour hot water onto the windscreen, dig at the tear, and it slips free at last. You sniff at its edges and catch just the faint scent of eucalyptus. They'll be going to bed soon if all is well, otherwise it'll be another long bloody night.

ANNA'S FLAGS

It was the little things, Anna thought. The ones you hardly noticed, like the single white hair that clings to your shoulder until someone like Mrs Darton tweezes it off. Mrs Darton was the middle-aged woman from the Catholic Fellowship who'd take Anna to Mass and check out her general well-being, like whether she'd been eating her greens, drinking enough, taking her medication.

Where were the keys? When they were on the sideboard, just beneath the hook labelled "keys", that was all right, but when three hours went by before they turned up in the butter, well, that was a waste of a perfectly good morning.

Recently, Anna Miller had been losing more and more perfectly good mornings, so that she even started to confuse the times she needed to take her medication. It didn't take long for Mrs Darton to notice, and when she did she was quick to suggest that Anna moved into a home.

Anna did not like the idea, although she knew deep down that Mrs Darton was right; but she prayed that she might just not wake up one morning before Mrs Darton came to take her to Mass.

Mass, or rather the Catholic Fellowship, had brought her Mrs Darton, who one day stood on her doorstep. A cake sale was on over the road at the community hall to bring people together and incite them to help the needy. Christmas was just three months away.

"You don't have to be Catholic to buy a cake," Mrs Darton had said. "And we even have *Schwarzwälder Kirschtorte*. Did you know that it doesn't come from the Black Forest? A baker in Bonn added the *Kirschschnaps*." She laughed.

Anna had stared at the small woman who seemed to be bouncing insider information as if hitting a tennis ball against a brick wall. "I am Catholic."

"All the better," she said.

"But I've lapsed, I'm afraid," Anna told her.

"No need to be."

Anna stroked one tip of her collar and Mrs Darton leant forward and plucked a white hair from Anna's shoulder.

"Afraid? You can always pick up again. Do come on over and look at the cakes." And she turned and waved in the direction of the community hall and the people streaming towards it. "No doubt the *Kirsch*," Mrs Darton said with a smirk.

Anna bought two slices of the *Schwarzwälder Kirschtorte*. One she ate at the coffee stand at the hall and the other she took home and put away in the freezer to have the next week after Mass. She glanced at the key rack and sighed. They were all there. But Mrs Darton had said she'd have to be selective, only take special things, ones she couldn't bear to leave behind, like the photos of her husband and son.

All week Anna went through her cupboards and drawers. Every day she would place an item aside. The six-piece coffee set with the blue trim. The wine glasses. She wouldn't need all six anymore. Hadn't needed them in ages. Like the extra sheets and tablecloths in the dresser drawer. She would attend to those later. She had time.

The following Sunday, after she had thanked Mrs Darton, Anna defrosted the *Schwarzwälder Kirschtorte*. She made herself a cup of tea, placed the cake on a plate and settled into the large armchair facing the front window. She began to eat. It was still very good although a bit soggy. She closed her eyes and savoured the dark sweet chocolate cake with its slight tartness of spiked cherry. Suddenly she saw a jagged flash in a deep red sea of flags. She felt weak. Memories swam into each other. Red apples and bows on a small fir tree. The scent of mulled red wine and cinnamon. Christmas smells. And then flags, and farewells. She saw long-buried mind shots of Rothenburg ob der Tauber, the small town in Germany where she had been born. Bits and pieces. Snapshots and mind blasts. Are they all mine, Anna thought as she felt her pulse quicken.

Anna went to the dresser and opened the top drawer. She took out a ball of tissue paper the size of an orange and carefully unwrapped it. She gazed at the red glass bauble sprinkled with flecks of white and gold that she'd bought on a visit to Rothenburg a year after her son, Bill, had failed to come home. The medieval town now had a permanent Christmas shop just off the market square, which sold ornaments all year round. She remembered her awe. When was that now? She started counting. Over twenty years? Anna shook her head. There were too many memories.

Anna wrapped the bauble carefully. There was no going back there ever again. She would take the red bauble with her, she decided. Red was Christmas. Red was home. As she placed it back in the drawer her fingers touched material folded around two framed photos. Red. And blue. Yet red. Anna slipped the frames from the material and sat down in her rocker with the two flags. She stroked each one. One for Doug. Vietnam. The other for Bill. She rocked gently.

Anna heard a tap at the window and then a voice. "Mrs Miller?" Someone was watching her. Anna remembered her first days at high school. She couldn't speak English well then. She felt people staring at her. It eventually wore off the more her accent resembled their own. But her mother could never get used to the staring: "They will always see me as German," she said. "You will be lucky. You will become them."

Anna stood and moved to the window. There was nobody there. She looked over the road to the community hall and then gazed at Mary Callahan's front garden which was laced with the blue and mauve of freshly planted hydrangeas. Anna had seen Mary Callahan plant the row of potted plants. "It's the soil, the more alkaline, the bluer it gets. You can make it so," Mary had said. Anna didn't know which way the soil was, but the thought of changing its make up just to get a different colour of flower seemed somehow unnatural, if not plain wrong. She wondered if Mary Callahan was watching her now.

Then Anna heard the doorbell and a voice. "Are you ok, Mrs Miller?" Anna opened the door.

Mary Callahan stood on the doorstep and smiled, buoyed by relief. "Get your flag. Come on over to community hall," she said and turned back over the road.

Anna stood in the doorway. People were congregating on the steps of community hall. They were dressed in long tunics with some sort of pyjamas; the men had beards and flat sorts of hats, their fingers fiddled with beads as if counting a rosary; some of the women wore black veils, others coloured ones.

Lovely, Anna thought. The children had black hair; they were well behaved. No screeching and pulling. They seemed to be gentle folk, Anna thought, but she couldn't help feel a tinge of bitterness. They could have been the people who killed her son.

Anna looked for her keys. They were not on the sideboard. "Ah, on the rack where they belong," she said aloud. She dropped them into her pocket and pulled the door shut and crossed the street to where Mary Callahan was waiting.

"Didn't bring a flag Mrs Miller?" Mary Callahan said with one eyebrow raised. "Doug and Bill would be right there with you." Her voice had a slight edge.

Anna stroked the side of her neck and slowly shook her head. Mary Callahan was too young to know.

"Take this one," Mary said and pushed a red-white-and-blue flag into her hand. "Hold it by the stick. Wave the flag."

She sounds a little like Mrs Darton, Anna thought and smiled a thank you. Anna remembered the euphoria. She remembered standing with her mother, waving the flag to bid farewell to her father in uniform, a steel helmet almost covering his ears. Anna was five in 1939. Doug had been in uniform thirty years later and Bill had been only twenty-four when she waved the flag for what she thought was the last time. But now she was waving it again. Waving it for her husband and son.

"Go home," they shouted. Mary Callahan's voice rang through clearly. Then Anna heard another voice behind her. "Go home, it's Sunday." Mrs Darton's hand was on Anna's shoulder, steering her towards the small group of strangers.

Then Anna saw the little girl. She was five or six. Her eyes were wide, almost frozen an instant before she turned her face into her mother's side. Moving away from Mrs Darton, Anna let the flag glide from her hand and crossed back to her house.

She trembled as she unlocked the door and her breathing became a little faster. She went to the dresser and wrapped the photo of each of her heroes in tissue paper, and moved them closer to the Christmas bauble.

She closed her eyes and remembered a little girl in a crowd in a small town in Germany, waving a flag in a blur of red.

BAKU

I am an old man. I am invisible, almost as invisible as my sister. My sister lives in the house of her husband near the sea, in the house of his father and his fathers before him. My sister is younger, younger than I am, but not too young to have forgotten Black January. For the sake of her daughters, she has screened it out. Her daughters, my nieces, they are our spring.

Lights flash in colours of red, white, blue, green and her daughters sing words unknown to me: *oh oh-uh-oh oh, woki po-po,....* They sing of love and they hum. They were down by the water bathing in light streams when bulldozer men came to the house. Men with mallets did not see their mother, for, as I said, she was invisible. She did not sing. Nor did she hum.

When her husband came home her daughters were still bathing in glowlights and singing strange words. In the rubble, he screamed; a young child called out, "Freedom". The police came, took the young child away. Him, they left

112

crumpled and broken where once stood the house, that of his father and his fathers before him.

On the television, *babushki,* no longer invisible, sing of parties to cheering crowds. Down in the streets young people sing freedom. Policemen come, lights flash their colours; the police leave the young people alone.

I think of my sister. Did they not see her because she did not sing? My nieces are beautiful in red, white, blue, green. I think of their father with no house to live in. Will the colours still flash when the singing stops? I put down the telephone, turn off the television. I am too old to learn another new song.

THE HOOK

"Come out in the garden. I'll show you how it's done. A wonderful sport."

I suppressed a smile as my father reeled my husband in to his favourite game—golf.

"The clubs are in the garage. Just a tick. I know there aren't many courses out your way. But once you're hooked, you'll find a place to play," he said.

Jim grinned over to me and shrugged: Why not? No harm in having a go.

"You'd be better off with a spade," my mother muttered.

"What's that?" Dad said.

"Oh, nothing." Mum smiled.

It was Jim's first visit to Australia and we were all on our best behaviour. Parents usually meet their son-in-law when he is still a fiancé, but somehow we had missed out

114

on that formality. Jim followed my father to the garage where Dad kept his clubs, bag, buggy, buckets of balls, brolly, shoes, cap, towel and rainwear. He listened to the litany Dad read him on the clubs and the distances they could hit: the woods for the longer lengths, the irons for long and shorter ones, and those two distinctive fellows, the pitching wedge and putter.

"You don't need all this to start, of course. A half-set will do. Now let's take this one."

Jim nodded as Dad, always fond of an exhibition, pulled out a club with a shiny brown head.

"That's a Number 1 wood," he said. "The driver. It gives you the greatest distance when you tee off—if you hit it right, that is."

Dad then took a small white plastic ball with more holes in it than plastic.

"It's a practice ball," he said. "Can't go hitting real balls around in the garden. It won't fly far, but you'll get the swing."

Jim was not completely unacquainted with golf. He'd watched it on television and had found it a bit slow for a sport. A sport for the old and wealthy, he thought as he followed my father to a small plot of grass in the backyard.

"A spade would have been better," Mum muttered again.

I sat by the open window, my back to the men and watched her pluck two paper-brown leaves from the potted red begonia on the table.

She nearly snapped a young green shoot as a deep howl hollowed from the garden. I turned to see Jim flop to the ground like a puppet with a severed string. He lay ajumble on his side, then drew his knees up to his chin, as if he were playing egg. I would have laughed had it not been for the moan that rocked forth from deep inside him.

Mesmerized, I watched my father bend down to him, his hands hovering over Jim's fetal form, the way he used to hold them over our campfires in the bush—close enough to feel the heat, but full of fear of getting burned. Jim rolled his back away and clenched his teeth in fists of pain. Dad recoiled, helpless at his rebuke.

Mum and I stood planted as Dad picked up the driver. He pounded the earth in rhythm to a chant of: "What have I done? What have I done?"

I watched—it was like a film—the motion slow as Jim rose to his feet in after shock. He steadied and stood there, strangely at ease, back turned, feet in lush ferns and grasses edging the cauliflower in my parents' suburban garden. He looked as if he were relieving himself—in broad daylight. This time I couldn't care less about Dad's concern of what the neighbours might think. I ran out of the house. The slow heaving of his shoulders was his only movement, the deep drawing in of breath, his only sound.

"Jim! Dad! What's up?" I cried as I dashed out to break the hypnotic song that seemed to hold them both in trance.

My father straightened as if to stretch his sadness and floated his arm towards my husband's back. Like a kite, half billowed in a steady force, Jim was anchored by the legs to the herbaceous borders of the vegetable garden where my mother had spiked old plastic practice balls on to the end of stakes as markers.

"I think I've changed your lives," Dad said as tears welled in search of a downward roll. "His manhood." The emotion, the tiredness of years, broke through the dam of education and control.

I stepped to my husband's side as he let out a deep long breath through puckered lips and zipped his fly. "It's OK now," Jim said and smudged the pearly sweat from his brow. "But, hell, did it hurt. He was showing me how to swing. 'Keep your head down', he said. 'Pretend you've got a fish hook from your collar to your crotch.' He was concentrating so hard...I should have moved back out of the way. 'Swing easy, hit hard,' he said. I never thought he would. His posture must have been perfect, he was on a high."

I watched Jim go through the stance and the motions, somehow bound by the spell of the game.

"On the down stroke, I thought he would stop, but he followed through. Luckily, I moved   just a bit...moved my right thigh forward. That was a bit of protection when he connected."

Dad edged towards us, his head pulled down as if still caught in the hook. His eyes were wet and the tips of his moustache quivered like those of a cat listening to the wind. Jim turned and caught Dad's shoulders in both arms and held him, almost held him tight.

"I'll be sure to step back next time," he said. Relief washed over Dad's sunken face as a smile tugged at the corners of Jim's mouth. "Will you show me the driving range tomorrow?"

Arm in arm, Dad and Jim came back inside, with me, a matron of honour, behind them. Mum smiled: "I said you'd be better off with a spade."

The three of us looked at her in puzzlement.

"Take a spade, dig about in the garden. That's exercise. Take up golf, that's exercise too. But you'll be buying the clubs, bag, buggy, buckets of balls, brolly, shoes, cap, towel and rainwear, and the tees, of course... Spade's still cheaper."

"But I didn't get hooked on gardening, Mum," Jim said with a broad grin and winked at Dad.

Back home, Jim found a place to play, just like Dad said he would. Every year, when we visit, our three children love to hear Grandpa tell the story of how their Dad got hooked on golf.

There are always tears—tears of laughter as Grandma sinks the final putt: "He'd have been better off with a spade."

THE WIZARD OF OZ REVISITED

Oz never really had a wizard, but it did have a couple of tin mines, lions in the zoo and lots of straws through which the children drank milk.

Dorothy wore rubber thongs on the yellow hot sand that led to the beach; her dog was a kelpie. She lived near the rainforest and kept her ruby red shoes in a box in her room for fear that a hurricane might whip them away. She never actually wore them, but she´d look at them under her blanket at night and watch them glow, and she would dream.

She would dream that the land of Oz had a real wizard, one who could do Harry Potterish things. He would make gold out of the tin and then prop up the markets so that her daddy would smile again. He would tame the lions and let them loose to play with the kangaroos, and, best of all, he would put chocolate into her milk drink.

One evening she peeked around the corner of the living room. Her parents were watching a film on TV. It was called Australia. There was lots of desert and cattle and an Aboriginal boy she fell in love with. In the film, people were watching another film like old photos. She watched the boy climb up on the roof and lie on his stomach, propping his head in the cups of his hands. He turned to her and waved, motioning that she should watch with him.

Dorothy saw a tin man, and a lion and a straw man. She saw a witch and another. She saw a little girl with a puppy. The little girl was wearing sparkly shoes. The film was in black and white, but the little girl's shoes were red.

Just as the little girl was about to pull on a curtain to see who was behind it, bomber planes flew low. There were flames and horrid noises and screaming. Dorothy closed her eyes. Her mother turned and saw her.

"Go to bed," she said. "It's just the wizard of Oz. He's got a bald head and was hiding behind the curtain. That was the war."

Dorothy lay in her bed and stroked her ruby red shoes. There was no war in the Land of Oz, she thought. And a wizard with a bald head isn't really a wizard. Then she saw the face of the Aboriginal boy. He smiled at her and he winked.

Dorothy sighed. He'll be my wizard. He'll make *thinks* better and true. She pushed the shoes away and patted her kelpie curled up at her feet. "Sleep well, Toto," she said.

THE WAYS OF LOVE

"Summer's gone," I sighed and set the lacy hands of the grandfather clock face back one hour.

Jack puffed on his pipe and the smoke curled upwards, sweet and thick, from the deep leather armchair. I felt warm and comfortable as I watched him run his left hand through his greying curls. "Something nice about autumn," he said. "Slow. Easy."

My gaze drifted around the living room; everything was as it should be. Of late, autumn seemed to ease into a winter's sleep. Yet I felt I should be doing something, if only to preserve a verve of summer. "I could start going through those old photos. I'll get the box," I said and ducked behind the heavy curtain girdling the alcove. Rummaging in the trove of paper memories, I came up for air, a peeling cardboard binder in my hands. "Jack, look. I've found my old scrapbook."

It was Jack's turn to sigh.

I pulled up the foot rest to settle at his knees. "Remember this?" I said

"What, dear?" Jack pulled his legs up and I rested my back against his thighs. "Oh, that," he said and grinned at the note creased in coded symbols. "How old were we? Ten?"

"Our first love notes," I said. "I kept yours."

"Well, it was tough keeping coded notes on me. Anyway, all the gang knew the code. Remember how Pete cracked every one of them. Got you mad, that."

I couldn't help smiling at the memory of a pigtailed girl in shorts racing to stow her secret messages in Jack's fleeing back pockets and still keep her place in the gang. I looked up and saw a tinge of colour whisk across his cheeks.

"And this one? The story you sent me when we were in our teens. You know, the one by Böll about the girl he refused to include in the count of people crossing the bridge. He didn't want her to become an anonymous statistic."

"Mmm. Let me stretch a bit. Did I really give you that?"

"Oh, Jack. It's not all that long ago." I smiled and nudged his knee with my back. "He had a point, you know." My eyes caught his, then wavered from his gaze. "And these? That's your writing." Triumphant now. "The letters you wrote while I was away—my month in Paris."

He ruffled my hair. I knew he knew I tinted the grey, but he never let on that I'd changed for him in any way,

123

even after twenty years of marriage. Twenty years—an almost lifetime together, just the two of us. I shut the book on the first half of our lives.

Jack was at the office. He had a quiet job—the Isle of Man did not stress surveyors. I'd done the housework and was sitting down with a cup of tea. I leant my head back and stretched my legs, kicking off the white terry slippers to wriggle my toes. The alcove stared at me. The papers. All those letters. The letters—they had somehow brought him close to me even while he wasn't. But now that he was close, I seemed to miss something. Funny, it hadn't bothered me before. I'd always had plenty to do. There was the house, the garden, but lately, too, a feeling—like the washing, waiting, waiting to dry.

It wasn't that I regretted anything. I'd had my month away. I remembered that month in Paris: oh, sure, I'd done the galleries, the bistros. I'd found new friends, gay happy ones.

"The Isle of Man? That's where you're from?" The girls would giggle. "Why leave?"

"The island's not famous for its men but for its stamps and tail-less cats."

"Cats with no tails," we'd laugh, the wine making it our favourite joke, bringing tears to our eyes. But I missed Jack.

I still loved him dearly. Whatever made me think that? Of course I did. "Linda, make yourself a cup of tea," I said. "Then get on with those papers." "Yep," I answered. I sat back down with my cup, my eyes following the steam as it wafted up to the high-beamed ceiling. Cobwebs up there. I saw myself, both feet firmly on the ladder, balancing the broom like a wand. I took another sip of tea. What if I fell? The letters. I loved to rip them open, such a thrill. Stop whingeing, Linda. "Guess I'd better get on with it," I said aloud.

When I went out to get the mail, there was a letter. It was addressed to me. "Mrs Linda Phillips". French stamps. I ripped it open to find an unsigned sheet of paper. The page was type-written. It was a fable about a dolphin that became a man. The whimsy of the story appealed to me and I puzzled about who could have sent it. I read it through again and then tucked it into my memory binder, forgetting the cobwebs on the ceiling.

The following week, another envelope from France arrived. It contained a poem about a bird in a cage. No signature. Then another, a love poem. The next week another yet—a haiku verse. No signature.

Who could it be? Someone in France? Oh, it couldn't be... No, not Pete, not after all these years. Well, he was the only other possibility, but we'd lost touch—and anyway, what would he be doing in France? I thought about filing the letters. Neatly. By date of receipt. But they were gaining. So I tucked each envelope into the binder. I didn't want to perforate the pages.

Each week another story, another poem arrived. I almost expected them. And if it wasn't Pete? I began imagining what this secret correspondent was like. His letters had become...well, love letters of sorts, in the way of love letters of old. I treasured them in silence.

One day, just after Christmas, a different letter arrived. It was short, typed, and signed. An old love. Then another. He hoped to meet me. Then more poems, short verses, snippets by Prévert.

The next letter contained a return address. It wasn't a real address. It was marked "J. Prévert, poste restante, Paris XVI". It was like peeling onions, every peel laid bare another skin. Should I write back? I couldn't tell Jack now. I had to have a cup of tea. I had to think about it.

J. Prévert. The poet? He was dead. Well, there must be other Préverts in the world. I wasn't the only Phillips. But I didn't know any other Préverts.

"*Dear Mr Prévert,*

I don't know who you are, but thank you very much for your letters and stories and poems ...". No, that wouldn't do. What was I to write?

"*Dear Mr Prévert,*

Who are you? I am a married woman." No, that was no good. Hell, who was this guy?

"*Dear Mr Prévert,*

Thank you for your letters. Thank you for your stories, your poems. Who are you? Linda Phillips" I'd just have to wait and see what he said.

The following week, my letter box was empty. I cursed myself for wanting to know. Someone was playing a joke on me. What a fool I was. Then it came.

"*Dear Linda,*

did you know that your name means beauty. You always have been for me, ever since I met you years ago. I didn't know what beauty meant then. But I do now.

Love, JP."

Years ago? I had to smile. It must be Pete. What a rascal!

"Dear JP,

Are you sure that's your real name? I think I know who you are now. What are you doing in Paris? Linda."

"Dear Linda,

I wonder if you really know who I am. I have always loved you. I would love to see you. Perhaps we can meet. Love, JP."

All of a sudden I wasn't sure whether it was Pete or not. Hadn't he gone to Australia? Or was it one of the friends from my Paris days. Could I have missed Jack so much that I hadn't noticed someone else had fallen in love with me? No, that was impossible. You just felt these things. Who was this damn guy?

"Jack, why don't we go for a weekend to Paris?" I tried to keep my voice even.

"Why Paris, love?"

"Oh, just for old times' sake. I missed you a lot when I was there. Could show you all those places I went. Don't you want to know what I was up to?"

"Dear JP,

My husband and I are coming to Paris for the weekend of the 20th April. You can leave a letter for me 'poste restante, Paris XVI'. Linda."

"Dear Linda,

Meet me on Sunday at 3pm, in the Jeu de Paume, by Monet's picture "Impression". Love, JP."

I shook as I read the letter. I hoped to have a clue by using the same postal address, but I saw no-one I recognized hanging around the post office. I felt like a thief, stealing snippets of another life.

Unease, a sort of fear, whisked at my heart. I would go with Jack—just in case. Slip away to the loo and double back to the Monet and see who it was. I'd have to follow through.

Jack and I wandered about the impressionist exhibition. It was getting on for 3pm.

"Jack, I'll just be off to the loo," I said. I hurried past the Degas and the Renoirs. Now I really had to go. Where was that damn "Impression"? It seemed like ages before I entered a large hall. I walked up to check the title, to see that I'd found the right painting. "Impression par Claude Monet". There it was—covering half a wall. Beautiful in its simplicity. The orange ball of sun reflected in jagged strokes upon the teal-blue water. I stepped backwards. With every step I saw more. It was if moving away from it made it more understandable, more beautiful.

"It was one of his favourites," a voice said behind my ear. I froze. My body blocked. I felt a hand firm and warm on my shoulder.

"Whose favourites?" My heart fluttered.

"That poet you're so fond of, Jacques Prévert."

I tried to stay calm, but my heart was pounding. The hand remained on my shoulder but I could feel its grip soften.

"It's beautiful. Linda is too, in any language." The words breathed their warmth into my hair.

Butterflies danced in my heart as I leaned back against my husband's chest.

BOIS DE BOULOGNE

Count Marcel Slavik, at ten years old, already had most pronounced nostrils that would flare at the whiff of anything from rotten eggs to frangipani. Frangipani, of course, was not common in the Bois de Boulogne, where the ladies who strolled there often exuded various odours, some even redolent of the exotic bloom. The Bois de Boulogne was just round the corner from Rue la Fontaine where Marcel lived with a doting mother and a father who was what one could call "absent", for his only presence was by day when he was mostly unavailable, except for the odd breakfast.

One morning, Marcel's mother sent her son to fetch the required *croissants* and *madeleines*. Marcel had already cut his milk teeth on croissants dripping butter in their fresh-from-the-oven state, but it was the sight of the milky neck of the pastry cook's daughter and the longing to nuzzle in the fragrance with which he imagined it might be imbued that led to a half-life of lurking at the entrance to the *Pâtisserie de Rue la Fontaine*.

So it was on a bleak evening thirty years later, that the Count entered the *pâtisserie*, now under new ownership, and enquired as to the price of the freshly baked *fesses* displayed in a basket on the main counter. It was not his habit to ask the price of anything, but nothing better had come to mind as a way of commencing a communication, if not communion, with the young woman at the till, a nameplate on her breast pocket that read: Madeleine.

Madeleine Poncet was flattered when the tall, dark gentleman—he seemed obviously that—offered to accompany her to her apartment a street up from the Bois. No, he could—unfortunately—not come up, she said. Not yet, she thought. The Count nodded, of course, and offered his arm for her to take. She told him that she lived with her mother, that she sometimes feared the walk home alone. And all the while, the Count breathed in the odours calling to him in the night air until he could resist no longer and, sensing a lack of resistance, nuzzled the young woman's neck.

When Marcel bit into Madeleine, it wasn't the taste of her that got him going, it was the scent released by his teeth sinking into her flesh that transported him back to the time of his youth when he would loiter at the gates of the Bois de Boulogne, munching on a croissant, his nostrils flaring in preparation for a never-ending lifetime of predominantly olfactory associations.

Madeleine Poncet, for some reason, never again appeared at the *pâtisserie*, where it was whispered that she had been spirited off to a better life, somewhere, with some Count or other.

FENCES

My daughter and I were planting bulbs in the garden of our house in France.

"Can I have a dog?" Maarit said as she smoothed the earth with her small hands. "I promise to look after it."

"It's a bit early," I said.

"But you had a dog when you were little," she said.

"We'll ask your father."

She nodded and carefully placed a daffodil bulb in the hole I had dug.

I'd told our daughter about the dog I'd had as a child in Sydney. Bambi was a dark brown Kelpie, a cattle dog. We'd rush off and tear through the scrub in and out of the tall eucalyptus, down to the creek where we'd splash in the water.

When Bambi was five, she died from a tick bite. I couldn't believe a tick could get a cattle dog; they were meant to be immune. I'd check Bambi almost every day, but by the time I found the tick, it was too late.

That day in France when my husband came home, Maarit ran to his arms. "Can I have a dog, Daddy, please?"

He looked at me and I raised my eyebrows.

"We'll need a fence," he said. "They can't roam around like in Australia."

I thought of the houses in the street where I grew up in Sydney, how the fences were low and white and the gates always open.

Barney, a golden Labrador, lived over the road. He'd lounge on his lawn by the large camellia hedge that separated his garden from the next. When Rex, an Alsatian, came from next door they'd take off down the bush through the gums and the scrub, play and splash about in the creek.

But that was Australia, that was once upon a time.

"We can adopt one," Maarit said

"We could," my husband said without enthusiasm.

"A puppy. Please. Please."

"You'll have to take her for daily walks."

"Yes!"

"Get a leash."

"Yes!"

"And you would be responsible," my husband said.

"Oh Daddy!" Maarit said and leapt up to kiss him, and then she gave me a long hug.

So we picked up a puppy at the local animal shelter.

"She's as black as liquorice," Maarit said. "I'll call her Réglisse. That's liquorice in French."

"She's a Labrador and something else," my husband said. "She'll get big and you'll have to watch out for other dogs."

"She'll make friends with them," Maarit said. "Just like the dogs in Sydney."

Last month we took Maarit to Sydney to visit her grandparents. We had to leave Réglisse behind, because of the six-month quarantine. When we dropped Réglisse off at the dog motel she gave us a funny look, then obeying the leash she loped off with that cross-legged swing, her tail drooping.

On the flight to Australia, Maarit was sad.

"Réglisse will be all right," I said.

On the way to my parents' house from the airport, we saw people walking down the road and some had their dogs on a leash.

"You said they don't have to be on a leash here," my daughter said.

"Guess things have changed," I said.

When we pulled into our street, we saw a Labrador lounging on the lawn opposite my parents' house. "He's just like Barney," I said.

"Is Rex still next door?" Maarit asked.

"Doubt it," I said.

Just then a young Alsatian loped up the next-door drive and over the road. She sniffed at the Labrador. The Lab got up slowly and sniffed back. The two dogs pranced and circled each other and then trotted off down the bush.

"Just like Barney and Rex," Maarit said. "Like you told me."

"Let's see where they go," I said and took Maarit's hand.

We jogged down the road to the clearing guarded by wild blackberries just in time to see two wagging tails disappear down the steep stony track. We followed them down through the grey-green bushes and the yellow bottle brush of the banksias, trying not to slip on the dry gum leaves that sprinkled the trail.

All of a sudden the two dogs came towards us; they stopped then they turned to lope back down the creek.

"They're showing us the way," Maarit said and tugged at my hand.

The bush was thick with eucalyptus trees standing tall like sentries. Red resin gleamed on their smooth grey trunks. Then we heard splashing and came to the creek. The dogs were chasing each other, deftly avoiding half-hidden rocks as they leapt in and out of the shallow water.

"Let's stop here a while," I said.

So we sat and watched the dogs play. Then they shook their wet coats, turned to us with a "Come on" look and loped back up the track.

"Time to go, they're saying," Maarit said and tugged me up.

By the time we got back to our street, the two dogs lay panting on the lawn by the camellias.

"Some things do seem the same as before," I said

Maarit waved to the dogs and we went through the open gateway of my parent's house. Then she stopped. "Why can't the dogs in France have their dog friends like they do in Australia?"

"Because of the fences," I said. "And the leashes."

"But they even have them on a leash when we're out in the woods."

"Guess they're scared they won't like each other," I said.

"They don't even get a chance to make friends," Maarit said.

Three weeks later, we were back home in France. When we collected Réglisse from the dog motel, she leapt up and licked us, whimpering, her tail beating a welcome against our legs. When we got to the house my daughter and I took the leash and walked the stretch up to the woods. Then we let her go. Back and forth, doubling distance, Réglisse sniffed and fossicked, then leapt into the creek, splashing water about. I swear she was laughing.

In the distance, we saw another dog coming. The owner, quickly attached a leash. We called to Réglisse and leashed her, too. When we got to the same level Réglisse strained madly and so did the other dog, a young Alsatian.

Maarit looked at me. "They want to make friends," she said.

The other dog owner tugged at her dog, trying to keep a steady track ahead after a cursory "Bonjour."

"Ours is a nice dog," I said, patting Réglisse.

"My dog is nice, too," said the woman.

"Shall we let them go? Make friends?" I said.

The woman hesitated. "They won't fight?" she said.

"I don't think so. Want to risk it?"

She nodded and we both let our dogs free.

The two dogs began dancing and sniffing in a slow circles around each other, then they sped up and Réglisse rushed off. She stopped all of a sudden to let the Alsatian catch up. They galloped and sprang and sniffed and wrestled, raced down to the stream and into the water. When they came out they shook their coats and pranced back to us as we stood chatting beside the track.

We said so long and with a wave and a smile went on our separate ways. The Alsatian trotted off after its mistress, Réglisse after us. Réglisse turned around once then gambolled ahead.

"See," Maarit said. "They just wanted to be friends. Just like in Australia"

THE SYSTEM

I didn't have a clue about roulette and had never been to a casino although for the last five years we'd been living just a few miles from one in the French town of Divonne. Jack had been there once or twice with his colleagues from work. Roulette was only a game, he said, and anyway, it would be a different type of night out for us.

"But I don't have anything to wear," I said.

"You look fine."

"But I don't know how to play and I'll lose everything."

"We'll only take 200 francs. If we win that's fine. If we lose, we lose."

"That's fine, too," I said. "It's only a game."

"Yes, but if you have a system you won't lose," Jack said.

"A system?"

"Choose red or black and every time you win, double your stakes."

"What if you pick red and black comes? "

"You have to stick with the one you choose at the beginning. Just hang in there."

He seemed to be taking this game very seriously. I kissed him on the cheek. "Sort of like always going home with the guy you come with."

"Yeah. Sort of."

I felt a little out of place in my white cotton blouse and blue skirt. Nearly all the other women wore cocktail dresses and some of the men even had on tuxedos. But, Jack looked fine in his blazer. The casino was hushed as we moved from one roulette table to another.

"Aren't you allowed to make a noise?" I said.

Jack squeezed my hand. "Just pretend you do this every day," he whispered in my ear.

I nodded, wondering if that was what these people did.

Jack drew me into a space at one table. The croupier's eyes flickered our way. Then suddenly, Jack put two yellow 50 franc chips on red. I held my breath. The little white ball spun than clattered to a standstill. My heart fluttered. A red number. I almost squealed. The croupier pushed two more chips across the table then looked at me with a funny smile. I was sure it said "newbie".

"I can't stand this," I said.

"Shhh," Jack said.

Red came again. My heart was thumping.

"Aren't you going to take them?" I said.

"Shhh," Jack repeated.

"*Rien ne va plus*," the croupier said as the little white ball clattered. Then it stopped. On red.

I wiped my hands over my thighs. The croupier gave me a side-long glance and smiled his tiny smile as he pushed the chips over.

"Let's try another table, Jack," I whispered.

"Not now," he said. Then he took two chips and put them in my hand. "You have a go," he said.

"I couldn't," I said. "I'd just lose."

"That's the thrill of the game."

The croupier gave me a long look. "All right, then," I said to Jack, "but at another table."

"I'm staying here. You go. But remember, keep cool."

I wondered if Jack's heart was beating like mine as I moved across the room. Two tables away I stood planted for what seemed like ages beside a dour faced croupier, watching the small white ball go round and round. Then, as if it was the sort of thing I did every day, I leant forward and put one yellow chip on the number 30. I knew I didn't stand a chance, but this way it would soon be over. The ball dribbled and came to rest on 29. I felt almost relieved. I stopped to watch, but the single chip in my hand was burning to play. The faces of those at the table were without emotion, their eyes fixed on the clattering ball. The woman beside me hardly reacted as the croupier pushed a pile of chips her way.

I leant forward and placed my last chip on 30. The ball danced over the numbers and I felt an arm on my waist. Jack drew me close. "I've lost it," he whispered. My heart pitter-pattered. "It's only a game," I said. But I couldn't look away from the ball.

Jack drew me closer. The ball stopped. 30. I squealed. I grabbed him. Kissed him. The dour faced croupier broke out in a smile and pushed a pile of yellow chips over towards me. I beamed at him then swept the chips into my bag, as if that was the thing I did every day. I was tingling. "Let's go home, Jack," I said. "And I'll teach you my system."

QUATRE-VINGTS

Twenty years ago my husband and I came to Geneva for two months. I had learnt French at school in Australia. My husband only spoke German and English, so I was drumming the sense of *quatre-vingt* into his Austrian ears.

"*Quatre-vingt*?" he said. "That's crazy. Four twenty. *Achtzig* at least is the same as 'eighty'.

"It's logical," I said. "Four times twenty."

Geneva had been the chance of a lifetime for us and a place where our mother tongues could meet on neutral ground, without one always lagging behind the other as they did when we were in Austria or in Australia. We intended to learn French—local immersion. My school French was so rusty that I felt we were both starting out with the same slates. Almost. If it hadn't been for the numbers.

One day near Cornavin station my husband stopped at a small shop to buy cigarettes. I waited outside as there was hardly room to squeeze in behind him amongst the stands of newspapers and magazines.

He came out beaming, two packs in his hand. "They're so nice here," he said. "Guess what the woman said when she gave me the cigarettes?"

"Smoking kills?"

"Don't be silly. She said to come back in September."

I gave my husband a funny look. It was the 20th of August.

"September. That's what she said."

"Do you think she meant it?" I said as I saw the woman come running towards us.

"*Monsieur! Monsieur!*"

My husband spun around.

The woman was shaking a small ticket. "*Il Faut payer, monsieur. Quatre septante.*" She held the ticket under my nose. Four seventy. *Quatre, soixante-dix* my mind chanted in the French I had learned at school.

"She wants four francs seventy," I said. "She wants it now."

"September?" my husband said to the woman.

She nodded her head. "Yes, please. *Maintenant.*"

Now, twenty years later, we're both fluent in French and feeling comfortable with *quatre-vingts*.

But last week I picked up a paper at my local newsagent's. A new vendor was there, she had come from the Valais. "*Deux huitante*," she said. Or was it *octante*?

When I told my husband that night, he just answered: "It's only logical. *Octante* is *achtzig* and *huitante* is eighty. And we have been here now for one fourth of that."

ABOUT THE AUTHOR

Sylvia Petter is an Australian writer based in Vienna, Austria.

Her first collection of stories, *The Past Present*, was published in paperback and as an eBook in 2000/2001 by IUMIX, UK; her second collection, *Back Burning*, won a Best Fiction Award and was published in 2007 by IP, Australia.

Her website is http://www.sylviapetter.com and she blogs at http://www.mercsworld.blogspot.com Merc's World—writing and ruminations.